Praise for *The Unfinished Life of Addison Stone*

"Captivating, original, brilliant, and so dangerously exhilarating that you'll find yourself addicted to the entire immersive experience. You will fly through this thriller, incapable of putting it down." **—Lauren Myracle,**
New York Times bestselling author of *The Infinite Moment of Us*

"Only a writer as fierce and imaginative as Adele Griffin could bring us the real story of Addison Stone, a true talent and a bona fide star."
—Daniel Handler, *New York Times* **bestselling author of** *Why We Broke Up*

"A beautifully executed and riveting novel from an extraordinarily talented writer. Addison Stone will haunt you. Hers is a story you do not want to miss." **—Courtney Summers, author of the**
Cybil Award winner *Cracked Up to Be*

"[An] intricate, intoxicating novel . . . This compelling story can be read on many levels, from a multi-voiced meditation on a brief, bright life in the Big Apple to an exploration of the biographer's almost impossible task: the discovery and distillation of another's complex self."
—The Washington Post

"An acute examination of a young woman's troubled mind as much as it's a mystery . . . That she remains an enigma, even at the fascinating novel's end, somehow makes Addison's death all the more harrowing."
—The Boston Globe

"A layered homage to the tortured painter, but also an exercise in structure and discipline, complete with pictures, paintings, media clips and more."
—Parade.com

"Addictive . . . Despite all of the photos and paintings and interviews, Stone remains an enigma . . . As characters debate the true nature of Addison Stone, they reveal just how little they know each other and themselves, and how much they project their own beliefs, fears, and hopes onto the world."
—The Daily Beast

"Resembles an in-depth article one might read in *The New Yorker* . . . A compelling fictional biography." **—Shelf Awareness, Starred Review**

"Griffin, a two-time National Book Award finalist and one of the best YA authors around, attempts something very different here: a *Rashomon*-like take on a young girl's life, highlighted by photos of the girl and her art, all in an attempt to put the unknowable Addison more within the reader's grasp . . . A terrific experiment, something fresh and hard to put down. It gives a sense of both the artistic temperament and the nature of madness—and the sometimes thin line in between." —*Booklist*, **Starred Review**

"This fictional biography of a visual and performance artist Addison Stone is compelling and tragic from the very first page . . . Readers will be fascinated with the novel and caught up in the drama right up to the end."
—*School Library Journal*, **Starred Review**

"A compelling look at the dark underbelly of the Manic Pixie Dream Girl fantasy . . . There's no shortage of romance in the portrayal of Addison, the brilliant beauty who captured all eyes and whose ghost still powers imaginations, but perceptive readers will see beyond the glamour to the simmering dysfunction." —*The Bulletin of the Center for Children's Books*

"Griffin's mixed media approach is fresh and welcome; art and photographs dot the pages of a compelling biography." —*Romantic Times*

"A fast-paced, engaging read. Tormented by mental illness or possibly the supernatural, Addison is an unpredictable and compelling central figure."
—*VOYA*

"An intimate and cohesive portrait of a complex girl . . . The whirlwind pace will have readers in its grip." —*Horn Book Magazine*

"A faux biography of a deceased teenage rising star in the art world, [built] around interviews from people involved in Addison's life before she died, excerpts from media coverage of her rapidly growing fame, photographs of Addison and her friends, and images of her artwork . . . Griffin offers incisive commentary on mental illness and the frenzy around (and pressures induced by) celebrity, especially surrounding young women. Defined primarily by the contradictory accounts of those around her, Addison remains something of a cipher even by book's end." —*Publishers Weekly*

THE
UNFINISHED
LIFE OF
ADDISON
STONE

ADELE GRIFFIN

For Felicia!

remembering Addison!

SOHO TEEN

Published in the United States by Soho Teen
an imprint of
Soho Press, Inc.
853 Broadway
New York, NY 10003

Library of Congress Cataloging-in-Publication Data
Griffin, Adele.
The unfinished life of Addison Stone / Adele Griffin.

ISBN 978-1-61695-596-0
eISBN 978-1-61695-361-4

1. Mystery and detective stories. 2. Artists—Fiction.
3. Celebrities—Fiction. 4. New York (N.Y.)—Fiction. I. Title.
PZ7.G881325Un 2014
[Fic]—dc23   2014009576

Interior design by Janine Agro, Soho Press, Inc.

Printed in the United States of America

10 9 8 7 6 5 4 3 2 1

for Charlotte Sheedy

"I want a brighter word than bright."
–JOHN KEATS

Photograph of Addison Stone, courtesy of Lincoln Reed

ADDISON STONE,
WELL-KNOWN ARTIST,
DIES AT 18

AP TOP NEWS JULY 29 AT 4:59 A.M. EST

NEW YORK CITY (AP) – The New York City Police Department confirmed that they are investigating the death of artist Addison Stone. Her body was recovered early this morning in the East River near the Manhattan Bridge. Initial reports indicate that the victim fell while attempting to plaster a billboard at the Manhattan Bridge overpass.

"We were on the bridge, and we saw her fall," said Michael Frantin, who had been out celebrating his one-year wedding anniversary with his wife, Ginny. "She was wearing this silvery-white dress. It happened so fast. Like seeing a shooting star."

Earlier that night, the young woman had attended a party held by Carine Fratepietro at her gated estate, Briarcliff, in the Hudson River Valley. Following an argument with one of the guests, Stone departed abruptly. "She was upset," said another guest, Alexandre Norton, adding that Stone had been in a turbulent relationship with artist Lincoln Reed, best known for works that have dealt with an array of political and social themes, most particularly chemical warfare.

A friend of the family, who did not want to be identified, said that Stone, who previously lived with her family in Peace Dale, R.I.,

ERICKSON MCAVENA

had occasionally talked about taking her life and had attempted suicide at least once in the past.

Lt. Keith Buschhueter of the NYPD confirmed that the 911 hotline had received several frantic calls just before 2:30 a.m. Wednesday morning. Stone was unconscious and unresponsive when they arrived, Buschhueter said. He added that while this was an ongoing investigation, there were no signs of foul play. He described Stone's death as "an unsupervised tragedy."

"It appeared that she was not wearing a proper harness, nor taking precautions while working from a height of more than 20 feet," he said. "It is possible that these actions were deliberate."

Stone rose to fame both through her painting and her incendiary public antics. Her artwork was sold through Berger Galleries, but she often painted in public spaces such as bridges, water towers and abandoned buildings. She was perhaps best known for the controversial *Project #53*, the theft of her own portrait from the Whitney Museum, which occurred earlier this spring.

Addison Stone had been awarded the W.W. Sadtler Grant as well as a grant through the Maynard Foundation to study at Pratt Institute, her father, Roy, told the *New York Daily News*. Her works had been displayed in galleries and museums in New York, Los Angeles, Europe and Asia. "My daughter had everything in life to look forward to," said Stone. "I keep waiting for her to call and say this whole thing was just another one of her crazy stunts."

Art&Artist

WHO BROKE OUR BUTTERFLY?
The Last Days of Addison Stone
by Julie Jernigan

"Who Broke Our Butterfly?": *Art & Artist* magazine cover. *Art & Artist*'s cover story on Addison Stone was the highest-selling issue in the magazine's history.

PROLOGUE

I MET ADDISON STONE only once. She had enrolled as a freshman in my creative writing workshop at Pratt Institute. There were only six other students in my class, and as a visiting instructor, I was happy we'd be such a tight group. Fifteen minutes into the session, I'd figured this "A. Stone" person wasn't attending. So when a girl skittered in, late and unapologetic, I was annoyed.

She was striking: tall yet delicate, with pale skin and dark eyes and two braids like a pair of flat black ropes past her shoulders. The scars on her wrists caught me off guard. She didn't speak, not even to apologize for being late. Perhaps most telling, she scraped back the only empty chair so that it stood outside the circle I'd arranged. When she sat, her paint-spattered arms dropped at her sides as if she had no use of them.

We'd been making introductions, so I started over for her benefit. We went around the circle again: a few sentences each about who we were and where we'd come from. When we got to Addison, she shook her head.

"I'm not here yet," she said softly. Startled, some of the other students looked to me for a reaction. Who did this girl think she was? I had none. I was thinking, *Who'd remember anything else about that day except for the girl who told them she wasn't there?*

BEFORE THEY LEFT, I gave an assignment: pick a memory and describe it in the voice of yourself at the age you lived through it. One paragraph or one page—no more. Due in my inbox by five o'clock on Friday. At 5:13 on Friday, Addison's essay hit:

> *I'm last. I'm late. I pull my chair away for comfort. I'm invisible and exposed. My words establish my walls. My whole life I'm two people. I am I, and I am Her. I've been asked to pin down a moment. But do I care about my past? Why would I want to look behind when I'm hurtling forward so fast? I'm mostly scared I can't catch up with me. I am always almost out of time.*

A moment later, my inbox pinged with Addison's next email.

> *I'm dropping the class.*

And that was it.

Of course I never forgot her. When I heard that Addison had left Pratt after one semester, I was disappointed, but like everyone else on the faculty, I kept an eye on her career. I silently cheered when her self-portrait was accepted into the Whitney Biennial; I was fascinated by her prank *Project #53*. Then by next July, she was dead. A brilliant artist, all that potential, erased. It was heartbreaking and pointless.

I'd been blocked trying to come up with my next book idea, and as I learned more about my former student, I couldn't shake the fact that Addison Stone's life had all the ingredients of a perfect novel. Ultimately, I have to credit Julie Jernigan's explosive *Art & Artist* magazine cover story "Who Broke Our Butterfly?: The Last Days of Addison Stone" for kick-starting me to dig for a deeper truth—as it hinted that either one of two famous young men to whom she'd been linked romantically, Zachary Fratepietro and Lincoln Reed, might be culpable.

Every time I read that single cryptic paragraph Addison had dashed off for my class, I wondered if in some way she'd been asking for me to find her all along.

I decided to go looking. With a year off from teaching, I threw myself into my research. I taped hundreds of interviews from people whose lives were connected to Addison's. Her story took me from Sag Harbor to California, from Europe to Nepal, and of course to Peace Dale, Rhode Island, where Addison spent her childhood. She began to obsess me. In every gallery and café, on every street corner it seemed there was another Addison doppelgänger.

Addison doppelgänger, New York City, courtesy of Adele Griffin.

I kept thinking, ridiculously, that the closer I got to her past, the greater the chance I'd have of stealing a moment out of time with Addison herself—even if we were only brushing past each other on a city street. She was everywhere and nowhere.

And as police reports emerged that both Lincoln *and* Zach were in lower Manhattan that night, and that neither of them had an alibi that would clear their presence at or near the time of Addison's death, I grew more curious, even suspicious. Both proved difficult to reach. Neither wanted to talk.

What did they have to hide?

This question became my central mystery to solve.

After months of sifting, compiling, editing, and transcribing thousands of hours of the voices that knew Addison best, this biography pulls back the curtain to reveal the truth as I see it. The acknowledgments that appear at the end of this book can't begin to do justice to the generous commitment of the many people involved—including those who wished to remain anonymous. I am also hugely grateful to the contributions of photographs and memorabilia, the visuals of Addison's world that allowed us such vital intimacy.

To her family, friends, fans, or the reader who is new to all that was Addison, I hope you find her here.

Adele Griffin

I.
HOME AGAIN

JONAH LENOX: I guess you could call me Addison's first. We dated when we both lived in Peace Dale, but I moved to Boulder, Colorado, the same summer that Addison moved to New York. She loved that city, the city that killed her. When they brought Addison's body back from New York to bury her in Rhode Island, I could almost hear her joking: "Lenox, can you believe it? Just when I thought I got out, they dragged me back again!"

I'd flown in from Boulder the day before for the funeral. I went straight to our beach at Point Judith. To the spot we'd always picked, with a view out over the sandbar. I watched the sky and water gray on the horizon, and it looked so real and endless, and I knew. I even said it to myself, "She's free."

The beach at Point Judith, Rhode Island, courtesy of Jonah Lenox.

LUCY LIM: I'm Lucy. I'm—I mean, I was—Addy's best friend. I knew her since kindergarten. She should have been my roommate, my maid of honor, the godmother of my future kids. Instead she died. July twenty-eighth. The hottest day on record that year. The morning of her funeral, the heat still hadn't broken. Hotter than a shearer's armpit, my Grandmother Lim would have said. Nobody in their right mind would have come out of their house to stand around scratching themselves in a hot church for a funeral. Or so I thought.

But as soon as Mom and me turned onto Columbia Street, we saw the cars. Hundreds of them lining the road all the way to the church doors, and more parked skew up the lawn and along the cemetery gates. Plus photographers, news crews, so many kids I'd never seen before in my life. They all stood silent, holding deep-violet irises, printouts of her art, that *Catch* elevator picture of her and Lincoln, the printouts of her paintings, candles, even teddy bears. And I remember thinking, *Holy smokes, Addy! I wish you'd been here to see.*

JONAH LENOX: I did some shots of Jameson in Sugarfoot's kitchen before the service. I didn't want to go. Addison was my girl. I didn't know the other Addison Stone, the one who the whole town was showing up for. But I put on a tie, even if it was a thousand degrees in the shade. I wore my purple stocking hat she'd given me. That hat—I'd run into a burning building to get that hat.

WILMA PLANO, mortician at the Allens-Plano Funeral Home and Crematorium: I've been preparing the deceased here in Peace Dale for thirty-five years. I've readied old folks, children, sometimes teeny babies, bless their teeny baby hearts. Most everyone in my trade knows there's only one trick to this job: make it look like they're sleeping. But in all my years, I never saw such life in a dead girl's face. She had a glow. Like she was playing a prank on the world, like any minute she might just sit up and laugh. I couldn't shake the thought once it came in my head. Scared the daylights out of me, if you want to know the truth. I thought I couldn't be spooked by anything. Turns out I was wrong.

HAILEY REISS, reporter for *The Times*: I was assigned to cover Addison Stone's funeral. It was a real scoop, because at that point, her death was clouded with rumors, with some fingers pointing to it as a final Zach Frat prank, other fingers pointing to a quarrel with Lincoln Reed and that whole love triangle. Accident, suicide—you name it, people were gossiping. There was plenty of facts-don't-add-up mystery around that night. So I wanted to see who turned up and who didn't: the friends, the enemies, the general freak show . . . I wanted to get the money quote from Lincoln Reed—who never showed.

Addison Stone was—and still is—hot print.

My editor also wanted us to capture some images. Like maybe a shot of Lincoln looking guilty? Devastated? Or Carine Fratepietro hugging Addison's mom? Or that exotic giant Gil Cheba, all wasted and strung out? Or one of those Lutz brothers drinking lemonade on a country porch swing?

The Times thought it was all our own bright idea to run the funeral as a style piece—but as soon as I got to the Sheraton, I saw the press. *New York Post, Vanity Fair, New York,* Daily Beast, Gawker, TMZ, *People, Star, ArtRightNow.* And I saw Julie Jernigan, who ended up writing that now-classic story for *Art & Artist.* So yeah, everyone. We were all vying for our place on Reddit. But they made us check our cameras. It seemed like every local cop was there only to enforce Addison's privacy for just one day. You'll never see any of those pictures, because they didn't let anyone take any.

Addison's funeral was different from what I expected. Here we all were to cover it, the spectacle of celebrity death—too young, too beautiful, too talented, too soon—who *wouldn't* want to report that funeral?

But you know what else? It was really fucking sad. Addison's people, they all loved this girl. You could feel it, too. The massive electric surge of mourning.

OFFICER SEAMUS RIORDAN, South Kingstown Police: I've been on the force fifteen years and never saw anything like this. We were called in, six squad cars, at about 11:15 A.M.—and we'd been briefed. Demonstration was brewing around a funeral for a girl who was some big deal. Nah, I didn't recognize her name. Jon Bon Jovi, LeBron James, now that's some famous folks. But plenty of other people must have known about this dead kid, because next thing we've got is a traffic jam off Columbia all the way to Peace Dale First Congregational.

Plus the crowd. Kids sitting on the roofs of cars. Kids stacking wreaths on fire hydrants and purple-chalking messages onto sidewalks and telephone poles. Kids wrapping trees in toilet paper.

We had the pepper spray, the Tasers, all that. Any situation, it's best to be prepared. But then we came to realize they were just fans. Harmless. They'd been denied access into the church and just wanted to be part of something. Like the outdoor concert at our Johnnycake Festival over in Pawtucket is how I always describe it. We didn't need backup—and when it did turn violent, it was a family dispute at the reception, and none of us were there, anyway.

I went and checked out her gravesite a few days later. Had to see it for myself, by myself. All the flowers were blooming in the summer sunshine. It was real pretty. You wanna know something? You could still feel that girl's spirit. You could still feel all that love around her.

Gravesite of Addison Stone, St. Martin-in-the-Fields cemetery, Peace Dale, Rhode Island, courtesy of Adele Griffin.

CHARLIE STONE, brother: I'm younger than Addison by sixteen months. Her only sibling. For the record, I hate talking about my sister's funeral. But of course I remember every single thing about it. Mom and Dad and I were in the front pew. Then our cousins, Maddy and Morgan; Aunt Jen and Uncle Len; Gam-Gam, who's my grandmother on Dad's side; and our Bristol grandparents, Gran and Pop O'Hare. I wanted to nuke the open casket idea. My parents were slightly insane on that point. They were so proud of Addison's looks. An open casket was the one thing Mom and Dad could agree on.

Mom dressed Addison all wrong. I couldn't stop thinking how Addison would have been ripped that this was her last outfit. White button-down shirt and a long black skirt she used to wear for, like, choir recitals in ninth grade. Black booties that she hadn't even taken with her to New York. They'd been in the hall closet for two years, and then Mom's sending her to meet St. Peter in them? Jesus H. Christ.

I kept my butt in the pew. I've got happier memories of my sister than her dead face on a lace pillow. It wasn't till I was alone that I saw through the open door all those other people. That's when I got it that Addison's funeral was big. Bigger than homecoming. And these kids were so respectful. Just sitting on the roofs of cars or spread out on blankets on the grass. I couldn't stop feeling their . . . presence, I guess. Like a humming on the walls of the church. Was this whole *swoosh-swoosh-swoosh* surround-sound group-worship heartbeat how it felt to be Addison? And I wondered if she could feel it then, too.

LUCY LIM: I looked at her. I had to. I needed to know that girl who was so wildly alive was really gone. I could still feel all those burning, smoking wires in her mind. So what struck me hardest was the calm in Addy's face. No more fear, no more panic. Her eyes closed and her eyelashes curled up like a doll's. The pink in her cheek and the shine in her hair. Nothing raggedy or burnt out. Just my own Addy enjoying one of her naps.

MAUREEN STONE, mother: I say it to myself. I am the mother of a child who has died. I'm in the club nobody wants to join. Lord knows, for months I couldn't even pull it through my brain. My daughter was gone. My daughter is dead.

You can't know what it's like, all these years. You just can't know the feeling of being mother to a girl who you thought might die every single day—right up until the day she did.

EVE LIM, mother of Lucy: If you could have seen those girls together! Best friends! Lulu and Addy, Addy and Lulu, they called each other, always, always. Lucy was at Addison's house half the week, and Addison was with us the other half. Later, when the girls were in high school, we had Addison over more, on account of what was going on at her house.

I'm a single parent myself, so I loved the company. Driving the girls to the Cineplex or Applebee's. Changing the radio, listening to them laughing all over themselves in the backseat. Good times! I know Addison turned into a different girl from the Addy-and-Lulu days, but when I looked down at her face in the casket, I could hear her laugh ring out in my head. Her smile was sunshine. What a beauty. She'll be in my heart forever.

LUCY LIM: After the service, Mom and I were zombies. We'd been in three days of straight shock. And as we were sniffling our way to the reception in the church basement, that's when we realized a bunch of media types had sneaked in. Every squirrel wanting its nut, and all of 'em asking questions about Addy—her sex life, her drug life, her mental state, her supposed past suicide attempts, and most especially, where was Zach Frat? Where was Lincoln Reed? I looked across the room and saw Addy's brother. Poor Charlie, this reporter was riding him like a dog. And I knew it, I was like, *Aw, hell, Charlie's gonna lose it on this guy. He's gonna explode.*

JONAH LENOX: Later, I told Charlie, "I wish I'd been the one to throw the first punch. I wish I'd done you a solid with that reporter." But the thing is, when I can, I try to stay out of fights. Sugarfoot always said, "You best not end up like your daddy—or I'll shoot you off the farm, too!" So that day, I was slow to burn. I'd brought my own can of Coke, I'd doctored it up with whiskey, I was keeping myself numb and on the sidelines. But yeah, Charlie and the reporter had a scuffle, and then it was an out-and-out fight—and I couldn't stay away.

Charlie's a big dude with a flash temper. And I even heard the reporter say, "Didn't your sister have an *arrangement* with Max Berger?" So Charlie was like, "The fuck did you say? The *fuck* did you say? Repeat that?" When he didn't, Charlie grabbed a ladder-back chair and pinned the dude with it. "Say it again! Say it again!" If you knew Addison, you'd never ask something like that. Addison was her own person. She didn't need some old-fart art dealer like Berger to make it happen for her.

CHARLIE STONE: Yeah, the guy said he was press. Jack someone. Jack Jerk-Off. Talking about my sister like they were buddies. Like he was devastated. I'd just been called home from football training camp down in Pensacola, and my whole body was ready to rumble. My sister was dead. My *sister*. The chair was right there. I know the story went that I pinned him. But it was more like I shoved it into him, and as he fell against the wall, he landed a lucky punch.

So I punched back, perfect connect. There's relief in a solid connect sometimes, you know? And then Jonah Lenox—"The Lenox," Addison always called him, he was her high school boyfriend—he jumped in. The Lenox seems gentle, but provoke him and he'll fight to the dirty end. So before you know it, everyone's yelling and pulling, and my fists were punching, pounding . . . but I was glad for the bruises. Bruises that showed, I mean.

JACK FROEK, blogger and senior staff reporter for *Last Call* magazine: Let me just say it: this funeral was full of scum. Townies. They'd have leg-wrestled each other for a dropped

Cheeto. Same kind of hicks that killed Matthew Shepard. And in my defense, I *did* legit know Addison Stone from New York. I could text her anytime—what's the plan, stone? And she'd tell me, like, going to hear DJ Generate do a "surprise" set at the Green Monkey, don't show till midnight. And I'd be there. I'd get a quote from her, take a candid picture that really wasn't so candid. She loved the power. *Last Call* always ran stories on her and got exclusive snaps of her, especially when she was with Zach Frat—he's Carine Fratepietro's son, you know that? Art royalty. When Zach and Addison got together, you couldn't even see for all the photo flashes going.

Addison cruised on that love. We needed her, and she needed us. She was generous with her personal life, like she'd do pieces for us for free, just for fun, on what she ate for breakfast and where she liked to buy shoes or her art supplies—she was what we on staff called a "mode-info." One to watch. At the same time, she didn't do any of that Facebook or Instagram kind of self-promotion. Because while she was perfectly happy to be talked about, she didn't want to initiate the conversation.

The big news: Zach Fratepietro and Lincoln Reed were not at her funeral. They were *not* standing in that dinky church basement with a plate of barbecue and Bisquik. Everyone else was there, though. Max Berger and the Lutzes and half the Broyard and Galarza family dynasties had all schlepped up to Peace Dale. But neither of Stone's boys! And I had a tip that she'd fought with not one, but *both* Lincoln *and* Zach on that night, the same night that she died.

Sure, my approach with Charlie was wrong. But that gorilla should be locked up. He fractured my tibia in two places and gave me a black eye. Did he tell you that? I spent the day in Peace Dale's hillbilly hospital, getting x-rayed. I sent the kid the bill, too. Fucker. Not that I expected it'd get paid.

Stone in Spring

by Christa Waring

Styled by Beverly Feirtag • Photos by Christopher Bacardi

Addison Stone is used to being stared at. I am staring at her now, and so is most of the crowd feigning nonchalance in the perennially overpacked Café Rouge in the West Village. We have agreed to meet for coffee before she zips uptown to Frost Gallery to see "a new friend's" opening, and Stone is prompt, which surprises me—though it probably shouldn't. Long and lean in black pants and a perfectly distressed charcoal T-shirt, Stone's model-thin good looks are at immediate odds with her cheerful decision to order an iced café mocha plus a double-fudge gluten-free cupcake. "Does anyone really know

> I'm young,
> I'm a student,
> I have a ways to go.

what gluten is?" she asks. "I don't, I just know you're supposed to banish it." Stone's sweet tooth is contagious, it seems. I change my own order, adding a slice of lemon cake to complement my green tea. But daytime desserts seem a fitting pleasure for a young woman with an outsized appetite for this city. Stone is having a moment, having blasted into our consciousness last summer with her painting *Talking Head*, the runaway star of the Berger/Fratepietro glitz-fest. We need to know more. We need to know everything. So who is Addison Stone? She is, foremost, an artist. "I'm young, I'm a student, I have a ways to go," she acknowledges, but even she seems to know this definition of herself is not quite correct. Working mostly in oil on canvas, Stone's painterly portrait style is both nostalgic of another era while at the same time dismantling it, as her swashbuckling brushstroke captures powerful, beautiful

(cont. on page 128)

LUCY LIM: The reception was emotional overspill. Addy's mom had to go lie down on the cot in the church office. It was way too crowded. I remember thinking that it was like the dark side of the same drama she and I got when Addy first moved to New York. Addy had invited her mom down just to show her that everything was okay. It was also her mom's birthday, so she took us both to dinner, and a movie premiere, and then to a late-night garden party in Williamsburg after. Such a crush of people loving Addy already, and all of them scrambling to be closer.

Addison Stone, Maureen Stone, and Lucy Lim, courtesy of Brian Bedrino.

Addy's mom loved that night. Me, too. It was magic. It was the chaotic opposite of the church basement. Although Addy herself would have been amused. I could almost hear her telling me, "Lulu, my funeral was the shit! Everyone came! There was even a fight!" She'd have eaten it up with a spoon.

JONAH LENOX: Late in the afternoon, I drove around all the places where we'd gone. My grandma's barn, our old school, the Cold Creamery. I let myself slide back in love with her all over again. I kissed her for the first time at Cold Creamery. It was in October. I bought a scoop of honeycomb, and we shared it.

We'd been sitting on the stone bench outside. Addison'd said, "I love eating ice cream when it's cold out. Double cold- ness!" And she swung up her legs on my lap. Her mouth was sticky cream and honey. I wanted to ask her a million things. All those personal questions like, "What scares you? Are you a virgin? What would you do if you had a month to live? What would be your last meal on earth? What does heaven mean to you? What one word would describe you?"

But mostly I wanted to kiss her. Kissing Addison made me hungry. I was crazy for every detail of her—physically, men- tally, all of her. I knew I could get closer to Addison than to anyone else in the world, even if she left me needing more. So I was relieved not to see those other dickhead guys at her funeral, Zach and Lincoln. The only good thing from that day was those two not showing.

MAUREEN STONE: When everyone was gone—when the kids who'd been camping out on our lawn had packed off to catch up with their own lives, and Charlie had headed out to be with his friends, and Roy'd slunk off to bed—my girl was still gone, too.

Do you know they never found a note? I've read that about half the time in suicide, there's a note. Addison would have left one. As a mother, I know that. I know it from the deepest place in my heart. So I just can't believe she did it on purpose.

No. I *won't* believe it. And yes, I do think it was strange that those young men were nowhere to be seen. Especially Lincoln. All day, I had an eye out for him. Hoping. But nothing.

How could I not have a thousand questions?

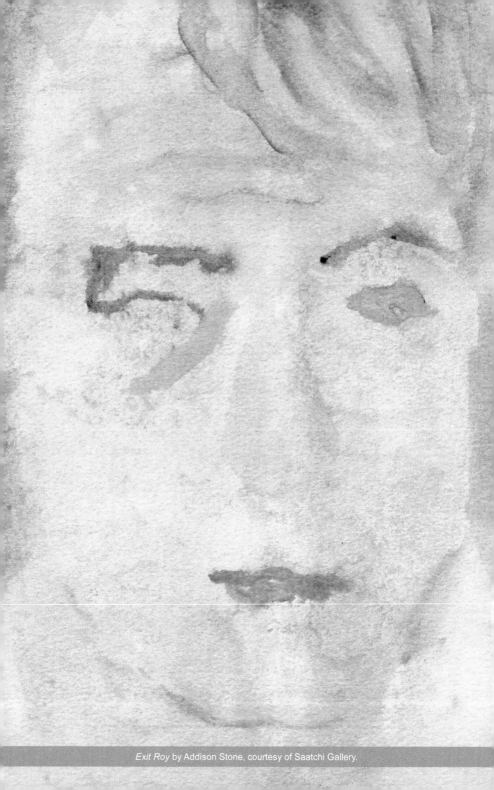

II.
GROWING UP STONE

ROY STONE, father: This is how I'll go down in history, right? As Addison Stone's father. That and her painting of me, *Exit Roy*. I hear it's hanging somewhere in London, England. I got no problem with a painting of me being famous. I just don't care for it. Maybe one day I'll go to London and see if anyone recognizes me. I got no problem with me being famous, either.

I'll give you the rundown on the family bloodline, how's that to start? My people are originally from Lowell, Massachusetts. Been there generations, working in the textile industry. Spinners, mostly. Cotton cloth, linen, wool, following the mills as they built them out along to Fall River, till that work dried up years ago, when this once-great country of ours got outsourced to India and owned by China. I mean, you can't find one thing in America that's made by Americans anymore, am I right?

When my dad, Ethan Stone, was a boy in the '50s, and even back when I was growing up in the '70s, there was plenty of mill and factory jobs. Most of my stock—uncles, aunts, cousins, everyone—eventually worked down the line at Burlington Coat Factory. My folks raised us three kids in Burlington and then later in Bristol. I was the smartass who went a different path. Earned my CPA straight after college. I was a damn near genius at math. Can I tell you something? I know for a fact that Addison inherited her art brain straight from my great-great-grandmother, Dorothea Egglington. Known by everyone as Dottie.

Dorothea "Dottie" Stone née Egglington, Fall River, 1913.
Photo credt unknown, courtesy of Roy Stone.

The way Addison could tease out a design, or how she'd draw a pattern or a shape to kiss your eye and make you think . . . well, that was Dottie, too. She was a legend—even looked a bit like Addison. "Black Irish," they call those looks. She could invent quilt and collar patterns—she was before her time. Now on Addison's mom's side, that's mostly strait-laced teachers, with plenty of flea-bit French Catholic nuns and Canadian lumberjacks. You better not tell Maureen I said that.

MAUREEN STONE: My grandmother, Addison's great-grand-mother, Renee Arsenault—she was the spitting image of

Addison. Not on the outside, but her soul. A real wild card. French-Canadian, a poet and adventuress, married twice before she met my grandfather. She traveled with one of those husbands all over the Great Lakes Region. Catching her own fish, living off the land—and then she joined a theater troupe in Vermont, the Portland Players. She was in a production of *Only an Orphan Girl* that was so popular it went on for almost a year. She was a maverick, Granny Renee. That's who Addison takes after. Don't let Roy tell you different.

Renee Arsenault, circa 1952 with an unidentified man, possibly her second husband. Photo credit unknown; courtesy of Maureen Stone.

ROY STONE: Once both kids were up and running, Maureen decided she needed a change from Bristol, and she began chatting up Peace Dale, the schools and hospitals and day care and on and on. Things that are important to a mother. I had no reason to stay in Bristol. Plus it never helps a man to argue with his wife, am I right?

So when Maureen found us the house with the white

picket fence, I rolled easy with it. Got a job working over at RoterMeril, in general accounting. The hours were tolerable, and the benefits weren't bad. At the time, Allison was just about five years old. That was when we called her Allison—you know she changed her name on her own? We named her after my mother. She got Allison from my side, and Grace is Maureen's mother. Allison Grace Stone. But I guess that wasn't good enough for her. Sure, it disappoints me. *Addison*—that's nobody's name!

Peace Dale was a decent living. Bramble Circle, where we lived, had friendly neighbors and clean lawns. First afternoon we moved in, you want to know what I did? I strung up a hammock. Like I said, I'm a casual man, I can settle in anywhere.

KARL TAEKO: My wife Ele and I lived across the street from Roy and Maureen Stone. They don't live here now, but the day they moved in, must have been fifteen years ago, my Ele starts stalking our yard like a gladiator. *"Ole wale, pupule, pupule!"* That's Hawaiian for, basically, "this shit ain't right."

"Aw, they're a nice family," I kept saying. "You've got your hackles up for nothing."

Ele wasn't fooled. Right off, Ele decided that Maureen Stone was a sorrowful woman. That Roy was too reckless. And the daughter was the worst combination: the dark spirit of them both. Ele even asked our shaman to perform a *la'au kahea* on our house, and she hung chimes on our porch to distract her mind from their crazy—the *pupule*, she calls it. Those chimes are still right out front.

Since Addison died, Bramble Circle's turned into a tourist attraction. Kids converge all hours to lay down flowers and votives, or they purple-spray-paint on the doorstep.

July—that's the month Addison died—was when we got most of 'em. Sleeping out on the lawn. They'll leave boxes of Marlboros and drawings and cards and vodka. Me and Ele collect it, and we put it in the garbage.

Roy and Maureen packed up and left 28 Bramble almost a year ago now. I know Maureen's living with her sister in New Jersey. I hear Roy's shacked up with some lady friend in a houseboat in Woonsocket. Ele and me, we're thinking of moving off somewhere different, too. The spirit here's been troubled for a real long time.

CHARLIE STONE: Peace Dale was supposed to be the Stone family's fresh start. Addison said even before I was born, she knew that Dad and Mom's marriage was shattered, and she worried about me. She said she'd babble at me during Mom's pregnancy. Press her mouth against Mom's belly and make funny noises to let me know I'd be okay. I don't doubt any of that. She was a real sweet sister.

I was four when we moved in, but Addison was going on six and remembered things. Like how Mom had a shit-fit because Dad had sent our stuff too cheap from Bristol. A mess of her wedding china was smashed. She was in tears, chucking the junk out on the back porch. Later Addison sneaked outside for the boxes, found a tube of rubber cement, and glued the fragments up on her wall in a mosaic. Took her all day, and she sliced her hand to pieces. Nobody watching, 'cause nobody ever was. Nine stitches. Addison told me she'd just wanted to make something beautiful out of something broken.

LUCY LIM: I'll never forget when my eyes clapped on Allison Grace Stone, out on the South Road School playground. The

Friday before, our teacher, Miss Katie, had told us a new girl was coming to join our class. I was batshit excited. I was only in kindergarten, and I had already figured out that nothing new ever happens at South Road.

That next Monday morning, she was the first thing I saw, galloping around on a pretend horse, making loud neighing noises, not caring that everyone was watching. She was called Allison back then, and she was obsessed with horses and unicorns—two things she never liked me to remind her about, ha ha. Allison Stone was skinny as a rail post, long legs and a chop of bangs just like me. But even then she had an eerie way of looking straight at and deeply through a person—and that wasn't like me at all.

Addison Stone, age five, courtesy of Maureen Stone.

She was so smart you could feel it come off her like heat, and I needed to be her friend so hard it hurt. In the end I guess it got tiresome for her, to have everyone always wanting her so bad. But she picked me that first day. She called me

Lulu, and I called her Ally—and that was it. And later, when she changed it, I called her Addy. I never even asked why. It fit her better, anyway.

KATE ORTEGA: I was Addison's first-grade teacher, "Miss Katie," as the kids said, at South Road School. We were a month into fall semester, and suddenly we get word that a child is transferring in. She'd been homeschooled, but on the phone, her mother assures me her daughter's the brightest penny I'll ever meet. All parents say those things. I just prayed she wasn't too far behind, or delayed. But that first morning, I saw the daring in that little girl's face. Her presence was older than her years. She moved through our classroom as if she were on a stage. She was already destined for bigger things.

I can't remember when, exactly, we did our classroom unit on favorite animals. But that was when she first drew something. It was a unicorn. She let me keep it, because she knew I loved it so much.

"How did you make this?" I asked her.

"It's from behind my eyelids, Miss Katie," Addison told me.

"What do you see behind your eyelids?" I asked her.

"The whole world. Only more of it," she answered. "There's a lot more behind my eyes than whatever's in front of them."

She won me over that day. She reminded me of a line from Keats: "I want a brighter word than bright, a fairer word than fair."

I tried not to see the other side of Addison—a darker word than dark. But if you were to ask me if darkness was in her, too, I'd have to say yes. Even as a little girl, yes. I saw the black opposite of bright.

LUCY LIM: From early days, kids were calling her Artist Girl. Her talent made her known. I wouldn't say popular—she was too freaky-deek for that word. But *known*. Plenty of kids were turned off by Addy's dominating energy. The way she told other kids their paintings weren't any good, or how she stole all the best chalks and paint-boxes, or her hair-trigger temper if "cleanup time" surprised her in the middle of a project.

But she'd give her art away like it was nothing. She had a flip side, always, that was generous to a fault. "Here, this one's for you, Tatum, because I know you love dolphins." And she wasn't even friends with Tatum. I remember how we'd all stand over Addy's shoulder and watch her draw. Me always closest because she'd picked me out for special. Have you seen any of her art from when she was in grade school? Holy smokes, am I right?

KATE ORTEGA: There wasn't a child in my first-grade class-room more gifted than Allison Stone, and I don't expect there ever will be. That first month, I sent an email blast to all the other teachers with attached images of her art. I wanted to give everyone a heads-up that this girl was extraordinary. Her cutout collages and her pencil drawings, even her watercolors were far beyond her years. There were *hers*, and then there were every other child's. Her mind was always a fresh bouquet of observations and conclusions. I needed the other educators to know that. Honestly, I felt it was my duty. Why? Well, because genius is such a rare animal. You want to acknowledge its presence, but you don't want to scare it off.

LUANNE DENGLER: Look, don't file me under school friend! I was never her friend. Addison was a bitch, and it wasn't just me who felt that way about her—lots of people thought she was selfish and a user. I know she's dead, but that's the reality.

Me and Addison didn't go to school together till seventh grade, when South Road School and Matunuck Elementary merged into South Kingstown Junior High. But back in first through fifth grade, she took ballet with me at Stage Door Dance.

Considering what Addison became, and the things she got famous for after she moved to New York, you'd think not being friends with her seems like a mistake, right? Like, she could have introduced me to actors and cool bands and got me into clubs and stuff, the way she did with Lucy Lim. Thing is, I didn't want to be a suck-up like Lucy. Because Lucy made it her *job* to take care of Addison, to be the full-time manager of Addison World. Sorry if I have too much self-esteem for that.

Besides, Addison was jealous of me. Sometimes I think Addison's negativity came down to how she didn't ever have any of the right things. For ballet, she had one old black Danskin and one pair of tights and a pair of too-small ballet slippers with the ties pulled off.

That first Sunday, I walk into the studio, and she's in my spot. Front and center. Anyone can see she's good but has no experience, ballet-wise. Worse than this, Madame Kuznetov has decided that this girl is her new pet. Suddenly it's "Miss Stone" this and "Miss Stone" that and "Miss Stone, you have flair" and "Look, girls, look at how Miss Stone is tucking in her derriere and how she's positioning her feet."

I wouldn't have cared, I swear, but Addison herself was always chafing me. "Dengler-berry," she got kids to call me— even Lucy. Addison could bring out Lucy's worst, especially when she turned into Addison's puppy dog.

Addison's mom got her lessons at Stage Door free, because she traded out Addison to do modeling for their website. Addison was pretty in a trendy way, I guess, and her mom wasn't shy about pimping out her looks. She'd do anything if it meant free crap. Look, I've got a baby of my own now. I get it that money doesn't grow on trees. People've got to provide for their kids. You play your cards. But Addison's mom didn't even try to be classy about it.

JENNIFER O'HARE MEYERS: Addison never called me Aunt Jen.

"Jen," she'd say.

"*Aunt* Jen," I'd correct.

"Right," she'd say. But she never made the change.

"Hey, Jen," she'd say, five minutes later.

My girls always called my sister Aunt Maureen. Charlie calls me Aunt Jen. But Addison never. She said Jen, on purpose and always.

When it came to parenting, Roy was the weak one. I say this on the record because Charlie's grown, and Addison's gone, and Maureen and Roy are separated now. You want to know the truth about Roy Stone? He was chased out of Bristol because he was seeing so many other women on the sly. He's a drunk and a deadbeat. Mostly a cheat. He's a disgrace to this family. I was always ashamed to call him my brother-in-law.

Maureen used to phone me in tears. "I found lipstick smudges on Roy's clothes," she'd say.

"Throw the bum out," I'd answer.

Then another time she called. "I found a lace bra in the glove compartment."

"Put a PI on that rat," I'd say. "When you divorce him, he'll need to pay through his cheating nose."

Finally Maureen got smart and listened to my advice, and spent the few hundred bucks she'd scraped to save on her own to have Roy followed. Turned out he was driving night after night to the same seedy Holiday Inn to meet his little honey. Maureen almost left him right then and there. But being that Charlie was a toddler and Addison not much older, it was a vulnerable time for Maureen. Roy never gave up seeing other women. Plus the money troubles got harder every year.

Of course, Len and I tried to help out Maureen and the kids. But my sister was too proud to take a dime. That's why she sent Addison out for those modeling jobs, and without an agent, some of that print work was pretty sleazy, in my opinion. But when it came to the ways of the world, Maureen could be awfully naïve.

LUCY LIM: In third grade, our school principal, Mr. Hemple, asked us to bring in food for the neediest. We all carted in jars and cans and sacks of potatoes, and this one kid, Jeremy Sullivan, he lugged in a whole case of GuS's ginger ale that was on overstock since his brother worked at Costco. A few days later I was playing at Addy's, and I saw that very same case out in their mudroom. It was the first time I'd thought of the Stone family as "neediest." Poor, sure. There were never any extras at Addy's house. No treats, no cable TV, no milk in the fridge, and sometimes the heat was turned down so low I didn't want to take off my winter parka. But *neediest*?

I never brought up the GuS's ginger ale case to Addy. She'd have walloped me.

MADDY MEYERS: I'm Addison's cousin, the one who was closest to her in age, but we weren't that close. I grew up in

Princeton, and now I go to UVA. My dad's a cosmetic surgeon. I'm not trying to brag about having a comfortable life, except Addison had such a chip on her shoulder about it.

One of my earliest memories of Addison's issues with my family was when she was about eight years old, and I was nine. It was the middle of summer, and Aunt Maureen had come out to Princeton with Allison and Charlie for a week's vacation. We'd always gotten along okay, but on that morning I came upstairs from breakfast to find her standing in the middle of my bedroom, wearing one of my Lilly Pulitzer sundresses. Her hands were on her hips, and she had a mean, harsh smile on her face. In her braids, with that smile, she reminded me of, like, crazy Pocahontas. To be honest, she scared me.

"What's wrong with you?" I asked. "Why are you in my dress?"

"It's not fair," she answered me. "You get to have your stupid, fancy private school, and you live in a big house with a swimming pool, and every day your mom buys you new things. And what do I have? Nothing!"

I had no idea what to say to that. I think I just said something like, "Whatever, you can't borrow my stuff without asking," and I made a move for the sleeve. "You shouldn't have touched *my* dress!"

She yelled, and she slapped my face. I mean, *really* hard. There was a cracking noise; my cheek was fried blood red.

I cried, but I didn't tell on her.

When they all left at the end of the week, I knew Addison had packed my dress in her suitcase. But I was too frightened to tell my mom about that, too.

The next time I saw her, at Thanksgiving, she said, "You need to start calling me Addison."

Addison Stone, age 8, courtesy of Maureen Stone.

"What?" I said. "Why?"

"Because. That's my name."

I was shocked. Since that's almost identical to my name, *Madison*.

Then she started calling me Maddy Maddy Maddy, and sometimes Mads.

Now everyone does. Nobody calls me Madison anymore. We went from Madison and Allison to Mads and Addison. It's not like I care that much; as Shakespeare says, "What's in a name?" It was more about *how* my cousin took it. Like it was her birthright. She stole it aggressively and for keeps. Same way she took my dress. And just like the dress, I was too scared to stop her.

CHARLIE STONE: When Addison started going out with Zach Frat, one of the first things she told me was that his family had six mansions, all over the world, and the one in California was a replica of a Japanese palace. She'd send me and

Lucy Lim these links to magazines where the Fratepietros were tricked out on their sweet yachts or with polo ponies. It was the only time Addison was ever awed. It didn't last long, of course. But I could see how a guy like Zach would knock you out, when you've hardly got anything more than the extra composition notebooks you get free from school.

Selected images of Addison's early notebooks, courtesy of the estate of Addison Stone.

Funny to think those notebooks are worth real money now. Not so funny that most of that money goes straight to Max Berger. That's a crime. Mom calls him "the hyena." He's getting some of Addison's designs manufactured overseas for his own profit, and I hear he's calling the clothing line "Addison Is Sleeping" since she always used to take a nap every day. Bottom line, he's ripping off her life and reaping the profits.

On the other hand, my sister's talent spilled out everywhere, and Berger was smart enough to see that. I mean, my parents and I had no idea. Berger knew. So what are you gonna do?

Max Berger, controlling executor of the Addison Stone estate, at his home. August Choksi Burns for *Art Home* magazine.

MAUREEN STONE: You could get a three-pack of girls' Hanes T-shirts on clearance. Addison restyled them. She'd deepen the dye for hours to get "her" shade of violet purple, and then she'd do something to the fabric, goodness, something I'd never think of. She'd add an exposed zipper, or a contrast double stitch, or a sliver of velvet, or a band of teeny-tiny safety pins.

I was disappointed when she could work the sewing machine well enough to take over everything. I loved sharing in her work—it was a spot of calm for us, as mother and daughter. But Addison said I slowed her down. Heavens, I couldn't take it personally. Everyone slowed her down. But she could have been a designer, easily, if the art thing hadn't worked out. She could have gone on one of those fashion competition television shows and won by a landslide.

LUCY LIM: It wasn't just art. Addy had geysers of talent everywhere. She'd make up languages, and then we'd use them, dozens of words and phrases just for us.

Like "snerps" meant a sweet loser. But "snerpick" meant a loser with attitude. "Squich," "squichy," the "squiching"—those were all different ways to say gross. We had plenty of words for guys, too—"sludgehut" meant a scummy stoner guy. And "lurchmeat" meant a gym rat, a dead-end dude like Mike Gandara who worked the gas pump at Cumberland Farms. "Boingzie" meant crazy cool, "froop" meant so stupid you couldn't even deal. "Cyclops"—that was about hurting for a guy so bad you were like a Cyclops, get it? Like, as if you had your one dumb eye perma-stuck on that guy.

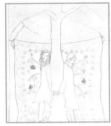

In middle school, she gave me a picture called *Friendship Quilt*. It's us under a tree, everything connected. I thumbtacked it to my corkboard, and every time Addison came over, she'd make a point to look at it. She liked those little comfort touchstones. Addison was more sentimental than she let on.

Friendship Quilt by Addison Stone, courtesy of Lucy Lim.

In both eighth and ninth grades, Addy snagged the lead in the school play—Dorothy in *The Wizard of Oz* and Mowgli in *The Jungle Book*. I don't think it was because she was the best actress or singer—although she was great. It was more that people just wanted to see her. On a stage, in the art room, in the cafeteria, anywhere.

For me, all that extra talent and charisma on Addy was like perfume. Everyone craved the scent, and nobody could have it. So instead people crowded her, sniffing her. I liked to believe that I was always able to keep my distance and yet be there for her whenever she needed me. That was *my* talent. I think that's why she never dropped me. I was careful. I had to learn when to attach, when to be in arm's reach, and then when to turn invisible.

JENNIFER O'HARE MEYERS: I'd always considered my niece too high-strung. Sensitive to herself and nobody else. But that changed on my husband Len's and my twentieth anniversary. I'd wanted to do something special, so I threw a party—a real bash, with bartenders and catered food and a jazz trio. I invited Maureen and Roy and the kids up for the weekend. Well, I had to. Maureen is my sister.

Maddy and Addison usually got along okay, and Maureen was being helpful, running errands with me. It was such a night, the doorbell ringing with more people every minute. We were all in the living room having drinks and hors d'oeuvres, when out of the corner of my eye, I see Addison.

I was speechless. All I could think was how on earth could Maureen have let her daughter wear that getup? A thirteen-year-old girl in a fish skin top, tutu, and spike-heeled boots? And did Addison ever know I was flustered! I'd bought my own girls matching ivory linen dresses with fuchsia sashes. They looked fresh as daisies. I think that's what made her walk extra slow, enjoying her drama, taking her time in these swaybacked steps. So choreographed. In one hand, she held a rolled-up tube—I thought it was a poster at first—but when she finally reached us, she snapped open the canvas.

"Happy twentieth, Jen and Len," she said. "I made a painting of you both."

You could have heard a pin drop.

I had to hand it to her; it's—I mean, there we were, Len and me, captured in a moment that I don't remember from any photograph, but to this day can remind me of when we'd just moved into our first apartment in Boston, as newlyweds. The painting is who we used to be, back when Len was in med school and I was working three jobs to pay rent. You feel our reliance on each other. You see my uncertainty and even my hope for our future just in the way I'm looking sidelong at Len. You can see his steadiness. His carefulness. It's amazing.

How did she do it? How did Addison know us, before she was even born? There's no photo of it that she might have copied. There's no answer.

When I got *Jen & Len* framed, I learned the dimensions: 38 x 51. That's a very big, expensive frame. But we paid for it, even with the museum-quality glass.

On that day, I realized that my niece, so exasperating—infuriating, even—also could do things that other people couldn't.

Jen & Len by Addison Stone, courtesy of Leonard and Jennifer Meyers.

MAXWELL BERGER: As Addison's primary art dealer, and the de facto executor of her estate, I am familiar with the painting *Jen & Len*. Hell, I drove to Princeton to appraise it myself.

Jen & Len is technically part of her juvenilia. Addison hadn't been studying art at the time. She hadn't come into her known technique. Essentially, she was a kid. But a genius kid. And that's why I had to eyeball it. She told me once that in grade school she'd seen a documentary on the artist Alex Katz, and the influence in that painting is obvious—seductive yet aloof. The smooth palate. It might be a work of art by a young person, but there's nothing childish about it.

I imagine Dr. and Mrs. Meyers are well aware that the hammer-sale of *Jen & Len*, if they ever wanted to put it up, would exceed the worth of their entire home and everything in it.

MADDY MEYERS: Mom would never say this, but Addison ruined Mom's and Dad's twentieth anniversary party. She made it so it wasn't about my parents at all. Everyone went *oooh* and *ahhh* and told Addison what a talented girl she was. Addison is all anyone remembers about that night.

LEN MEYERS: She stole my Rolex that same weekend, I'm pretty sure. She was a little cutpurse, that kid. I could never prove it. But anyway, it's a great painting. I'd have bought it for some real money. And now it's worth more than I could afford.

CHARLIE STONE: My sister started to make cash from her art in ninth grade. She was a hustler. She set up an art stand every Saturday in front of the Peace Dale movie theater. "Ten bucks a drawing! Come get the best doodle of yourself you'll ever own!" Then to me, she was like, "Go get me some business, Charlie, and I'll give you 10 percent." And I'd do it, too. Addison was fair to the point of over-generous. Usually she paid me about a 25 percent split on the profit if I could pull in buyers.

Addison could get your likeness down in five seconds. More like a portrait than a doodle, but she called them doodles, I think to show that she didn't take them too seriously. So nobody'd crap all over her if they didn't look right.

everyone wants you,
but you want my shoes

But damn, they looked perfect. Then she'd scribble a random note at the bottom. I actually kept a couple of them, ones she decided were mess-ups but were funny to me. "Everyone wants you, but you want my shoes," or "I'm less awake today," or "I've got a secret that is also a plan."

She made real coin till the cops shut her ass down. She had no license, and she was earning over two hundred bucks a day. Way more bank than your average lemonade stand.

I've got a secret
that's also a plan

Sketches by Addison Stone,
courtesy of the estate of
Addison Stone.

LUCY LIM: Addy would never babysit or wash cars or do bake sales or chores or any kid jobs. She earned money by entering art contests. There was this one time when we all had to draw a bicycle for art class freshman year. Addy's was so incredible that our principal wanted her to donate it, to be on permanent display in the South Kingstown hall. Addy said no donation, thank you very much. If the school wanted it, then it would cost a hundred dollars. And you know what? The school paid up.

Bike by Addison Stone, courtesy of South Kingstown High School.

She needed money so that she could buy top-of-the-line art supplies. But as soon as she had what she needed, she was stupid with her cash—like she'd blow it on some designer jacket or super-expensive gifts. She loved to come sweeping in with presents. She bought my mom bouquets of roses—for her birthday, Mother's Day, Valentine's. Once she bought me a Navajo fringe bag I'd been coveting from this vintage shop we loved over in Providence, and another time she got me a pair of moonstone earrings.

Of course when it came to gifts and Addy, you had to be careful. There was always a chance she'd stolen it. She was a bandit, the queen of the five-finger discount. "A clean heist is art," she'd say. I think that's why she loved crime movies—*Ocean's 11*, the James Bonds and Elmore Leonards. Where bad behavior looks cool and slick.

CHARLIE STONE: Have you ever talked to Lucy Lim about Green Hall? I've got my version. It was fall, I was thirteen, so Addison and Lucy must have been fifteen.

Green Hall is one of the Rhode Island Mansion museums. There's a mess of 'em over the Newport Bridge. The Elms, The Breakers, Green Hall, Marble House. A museum tour is not my idea of party time, but Mom was like, "I've got free promotional tickets. Let's go." Mom loved freebies. It was March, and it was cold. All we had to pay for was gas and restaurant lunch. Addison invited Lucy, and then Dad wanted in, too—mostly because he never liked it when Mom drove the car alone.

When Addison finally jumped in the car, she was wearing black tights and a black T-shirt, like a burglar. I knew something was up. She didn't talk at all, just *mmm*ed under her breath, which she did when she was thinking crazy. Like last time she *mmm*ed that way, maybe a year ago, she'd painted the word LAND in orange paint on our roof. She said she wanted to see if anything would land there.

When we got to Green Hall, she disappeared.

LUCY LIM: We kept looking around, but we couldn't leave the tour group. I was annoyed that she'd slipped us. I mean, who wants to hang out with your friend's weird family without your friend?

Addy's mom was scared, and I didn't get why. Addy vamoosed a lot. Like we'd be watching TV at my house, and she'd say she was going up to get a glass of water, and an hour later I'd find her taking a nap in my bed, or in the kitchen gossiping with my mom, or out on our patio, making chalk drawings—Mom always kept a box of sidewalk chalk out there for fun.

So no, I wasn't panicking. I figured she'd ditched to grab some sleep in the car. That would have been a standard Addy move. She could nap anywhere. But Addy's mom was more suspicious.

Addison at the Lim house, making a chalk drawing, courtesy of Eve Lim.

MAUREEN STONE: As the minutes ticked by, good Lord, yes, I became nervous. The tour was ending, and we were heading back from the bedrooms, down the sweeping staircase to the entrance hall. Addison liked to get lost; I knew that. The circus, the playground, a shopping mall. Then you'd find her splashing in the penny fountain or strolling near the animal cages. She was a mother's nightmare that way.

Once we were all in the main hall, and I heard the commotion from above, I had this dread, sixth-sense knowledge that it was Addison, and it was trouble.

ROY STONE: Everyone gets the joke of Green Hall, right? That Errol Flynn once stayed in that mansion, and he was famous for swinging from the chandelier? Addison was recreating it. For laughs. End of story.

LUCY LIM: Literally. Swung. From the chandelier. Two hundred pounds of lights and crystal, and Addy was just riding it like an electric horse. No harness, no rope. I remember she had on this purple stocking cap, like an elf hat. This was Addy, as insane and dangerous as I'd ever seen her. The noise was unbearable, too, a creaking, haunting groaning, and crystal prisms kept falling off and smashing to the black-and-white marble floor. If the cord hadn't been strong enough, Addy would have smashed to the floor, too.

Later I asked her, "Weren't you terrified? Didn't you think about how gruesome it would be to die that way?"

And she said, "Lulu, you worrywart, I never think about death. Death just Is."

We watched the clip go viral on YouTube, and that was cool. The boingziest boingzjob, we called it. When Addy moved down to New York, she first got known as "Chandelier Girl." Since then, truckloads of people have asked me, "What was that like, to see Addison do that live? To be in that instant with her?"

You want the honest answer? It was like being drunk on fear.

ZACH FRATEPIETRO: The chandelier video was my introduction to Addison Stone. I met Addison right when she first moved to New York, but I'd seen the clip before; everyone had. In the art world, it made a small splash. First time I brought Addison to dinner to meet my mother, Carine, that's how I introduced her. "Presenting Chandelier Girl." One of those rare times when my mother seemed impressed. Addison told me it was her tribute to Edgar Allan Poe. Her class was reading *The Pit and the Pendulum*. Pretty funny, right?

MADDY MEYERS: My cousin liked to break rules. Whatever high-concept garbage Addison was selling about the chandelier episode, the Poe homage or the Errol Flynn reboot, *please*—she did it for the rush and the fame. Addison pulled that stunt, and any other stunt, because the one thing she believed in was No Rules, Ever. She thought people should always do exactly what they wanted. She did it to do it. She did it because it felt good. I will just say that after that day, nobody ever called her Allison again, even by mistake. Not even my mom, who'd always felt like if Addison couldn't even call her "Aunt" Jen, then she sure wasn't going to call her some new, self-adopted name. But the chandelier was like a baptism by fire. After that, we all realized that Addison was playing for a bigger theater than just friends and family. That was the day she became Addison, forever.

LUCY LIM: Future Addy sprang into motion that day. Green Hall had everything that inspired her. It was shock and beauty and Addy at the center. It was Addy who got that video to go viral, too. She was controlling the hell out of her image, even back then, before she had an image to control.

STEVEN JOHANNES: Addison listed an ad in the RISD classifieds, and she paid me cash, and I filmed it with my own camera—*so it's not copyright infringement.* You hear that, Max Berger, you asshole? Berger sends me legal letters from time to time. He says that clip is part of the Addison Stone estate. It's not and he can suck it.

Chandelier Girl is still my most downloaded bit. People ask me about it all the time. I was thinking about doing something for the ten-year anniversary of it, especially with Addison becoming so famous since she died. No disrespect.

Addison had specific instructions. She'd thought it all out ahead, which was another reason I hadn't counted on her being a kid. I remember she texted something like, Be at the

Green Hall mansion at 1 p.m., wait for me to show, we will meet briefly, then you will wait for me to give the signal to film. Cash up front. Half pay if security interferes. With a map of exactly where to meet. If I'd known I was taking orders from a teenager, I'd have never shown. Although she wasn't "Addison Stone" yet, right? She was just some wacky chick.

"So what's your film?" I asked her when we met.

"I'm riding the Green Hall chandelier."

"You test it yet?" I asked.

"No. That's the thriller part. It might not hold." Then she asked if I was still in—since it wasn't legal, what we were doing. Or even smart. Or sane. So there was all that risk. I was in. I was worried, but I needed the cash—and she had it.

We set up the shot. It'd have to be one take, obviously.

She said, "Keep filming even if it drops."

I was like, "If it drops, kiddo, you will die."

And she was like, "Exactly. And if I die, you need to make that death worth watching."

Who could forget a girl saying something as bleak as that?

LUCY LIM: People think of Green Hall as the gateway stunt, right? Addy was transitioning from a round-eyed, "Look at me, I can sing and draw and paint and dance" art-room girl into the daredevil icon that we made into a T-shirt.

That's what I think is the deep-mineral core of all Addy's messages. People can get into bigger thoughts, like *BRKLN*'s "Personal Exuberance of the Anarchist" article that came out a few years later. But Green Hall was a rush in her ears. It was the beginning of something.

Except that the "exuberant anarchy" of Green Hall wasn't the gateway stunt, after all. Because after that, Addy lost her mind and everything fell apart.

BRKLN

The Personal Exuberance of the Anarchist

Jacob Rilleau
interviews local artist
ADDISON STONE

LADY KILLS/*RIP* WILLIAMSBURG
8 TRENDS WE REALLY, REALLY, *REALLY* HATE
ARTISTS TO WATCH/MERMAID PARADE

"The Personal Exuberance of the Anarchist": *BRKLN* magazine cover.

III.
"SHE LOOKED LIKE A SKELETON IN A T-SHIRT."

MAUREEN STONE: After Newport, I began to watch my daughter extra carefully. Goodness, I had to. I was a nervous wreck. She'd always been an unpredictable girl, but what she'd done that day wasn't just a prank, or a teen being quirky. It was a wildness inside her. I couldn't understand it.

Addison never got caught, and so she never had to come clean about that day at Green Hall. But I was so relieved she'd lived through it, I couldn't get up the energy to be angry about it. So I never punished her.

In the video, her body looks as close to free as I imagine my girl ever got. But for years, I had a recurring nightmare where I saw Addison smashing from twenty feet onto a marble floor. I saw her broken neck and her twisted limbs. Over and over I woke up in a sweat from this terrible dream.

And of course, in the end, she did die in a fall. It was as if my maternal instinct knew bits and pieces of her fate already.

ROY STONE: People make too much about Green Hall. Want to know what I said to Maureen? Addison was on something. Meth? Ecstasy? Stoned? Hard to say. But I'd bet every gold filling in my mouth that she was high as a kite.

The O'Hare home, Dartmouth, Massachusetts, courtesy of Nancy O'Hare.

MAUREEN STONE: Addison's father wasn't around enough to see the real Addison. "Kids will be kids," he'd say. As if that meant anything. And when Roy was watching, he only saw what he wanted. Green Hall wasn't even the worst of it. The real darkness fell the next year—the summer before eleventh grade.

MADDY MEYERS: The way I see it, Addison's serious problems started on North Lyn. In July our moms always liked to go to our grandparents' house, which is actually outside Bristol proper, up in Dartmouth, Massachusetts. Not much fun. The whole time we're out there, Mom and Aunt Maureen turn into these teenager versions of themselves. Mousy, obedient Irish Catholic daughters.

Addison and I got along better there than we did anywhere else. We would talk about how spineless our moms could turn in that house. How they made us obey all the O'Hare house rules, no questions asked. "Get up, it's time for mass! Make your bed with hospital corners! Finish your plate; children are starving in India!"

Gran and Pops didn't push Addison too hard. She had an

ease with them, like she didn't mind spending an afternoon bird-watching with Pops or learning how to make a home-made pastry crust with Gran. She was a natural at one-on-one. Sometimes I think it's what made her good at doing people's portraits. Her attentiveness, you know? So if she didn't finish her broccoli, they were softer her, they'd look the other way.

That summer, Charlie was up in New Hampshire at an all-boys' camp, Camp Winnipsaukee. And my older sister, Morgan, was an au pair in Nantucket. So it was just us in the country, bored and relying on our moms to drive us places, not knowing anybody. Addison and I shared our mothers' old room. Twin beds with lumpy mattresses that felt like you were sleeping on a pile of socks.

Starting the very first night, she couldn't sleep. "Gimme your iPad," she'd say, because she didn't have her own.

Sometimes she'd get nightmares, and she'd squeeze into bed with me. Her skinny arms would be wrapped around me, tight as locking pliers. I kind of liked it. It meant we were still close, cousins-close, and if she needed to squeeze up to me to get sleep, I let her. It meant she needed me.

Then one night it was different. She shook me awake—so hard her nails were biting my skin, and her voice was hissing.

"Maddy, listen, listen! Can you hear it, too? Can you hear them? Can you hear the people in the wall?"

I snapped on the lamp. I heard nothing. I told her she was freaking me out.

"Come on! Can't you hear it, Maddy?" she kept asking. "I'm listening through time! I'm hearing conversation left-overs from dead people."

"Stop it! Stop scaring me! There's nobody in the wall, Addison!" I shoved her away.

She started pacing. "Miss Cal is having soft-boiled eggs for lunch, and Douglas, he's going into town later to fetch his boots; they were being re-soled. Ida wants him to bring her back a bag of butterscotch and some new paintbrushes."

I thought it was some prank she was playing. "Shut up!" I told her. "Shut up, shut up, shut up!"

But she didn't stop. She kept on telling me what she could hear through the wall, repeating conversations she swore were real.

Eventually I got it. These voices *were* real. To her.

JENNIFER O'HARE MEYERS: My sister called in a shrink.

I said, "Connect with somebody, do something. Do whatever it takes, Maureen. But don't do this alone, and don't get Roy involved. First he'll say everyone's overreacting. Then he'll gripe about the medical bills." That was my advice.

DR. EVELYN TUTTNAUER: I took on Addison's case immediately. I became her primary psychiatrist. I'd been referred through Maureen Stone's general physician, Dr. Fergis, who contacted me in mid-July. He told me his patient, Maureen, was agitated about her sixteen-year-old daughter. According to his patient, Addison Stone was having chronic auditory hallucinations; she believed she could hear voices through the walls of her grandparents' house.

With no medical history, I assumed that the young woman wasn't delusional but was just acting out. Sometimes patients, young patients especially, invent voices or outside forces as a means to express their own desires or needs. It's hard to say, "Pay attention to me." It's easier to invent some monkey business that forces people to pay attention. And I knew her home life was troubled.

I Skyped briefly with Addison. In spite of her exhausted and disheveled appearance, she didn't strike me as someone suffering from any particular neurological disorder. My hunch was that she'd internalized some resentment for her brother, who she told me was having lots of fun at his sleepaway camp. This resentment was manifesting as a pseudo-hallucinatory syndrome. I noted after the Skype call that even in her bedraggled state, Addison Stone was charismatic and engaging, and that our call could have been a kind of inventive "notice me" performance.

Still, I advised Maureen and her husband to keep strict watch over their daughter. I advised Addison to take vitamins, and I prescribed a gentle sleep aid. We scheduled a doctor's visit at the end of July in my office in Providence.

Of course if we'd met in person, I'd probably have recommended in-patient treatment combined with a course of antipsychotic medication. Unfortunately, I'm not psychic. I don't regard myself as culpable for what happened in the ensuing weeks. One Skype session is not enough. If Addison's mother was truly in a red-alarm state of worry, she should have brought Addison right to me.

MADDY MEYERS: She was like a ghoul. She was listening at walls nonstop, keeping lights on all night. Addison had spent her whole life frightening me, but this was different. Because this time, *she* was frightened, too. But after the doctor said Addison was making up voices because she was jealous of Charlie—which made no sense—our moms treated it all like a prank, like what she'd done at Green Hall.

"Are you *sure* you hear people talking, Addison? Or do you just want to liven things up around here?"

Or "Will you tell the ghosts to be quiet? It's after ten

o'clock, time for bed, naughty ghosties!" That's always been the problem with our moms—they're Catholic schoolgirls. Obedient. If a priest or a doctor says it's true, then it's true.

But Addison began to detach. Like, hiding her food in her napkin. Staring into space, pinching the insides of her arms, pretending to watch TV—when she was actually looking past it, waiting for voices from Miss Cal or Douglas or especially the girl who was our age, Ida. She told me all this creepy stuff. She said she could feel three time-layers of the same house crimped up together. She said every family was living here at once, only they couldn't see us and we couldn't see them. Ida and Ida's people were the loudest voices, she told me.

Then Addison started drawing pictures of the "original layer," as she called it. Ida's layer. She said the dining room used to be half the size, because there'd been a pantry. She'd drink coffee and draw these ugly pencil sketches of Ida. She'd tape the drawings up to the fridge or to the medicine cabinet in our bathroom. I hated those pictures. I tore them all up. Now I wish I hadn't, for all kinds of reasons.

And you can imagine how well the "haunted house" idea was going down with our super-religious grandparents, right? They thought Addison was bringing something evil inside. Not intentionally, of course, but my grandparents are church-going people, and they couldn't handle Addison's "ghosts." Luckily, Aunt Maureen was smart enough to pack Addison up and take her home before they asked them to leave.

MAUREEN STONE: When Charlie got that sports camp scholarship, it was a wonderful thing. We all celebrated it. Addison, too. Addison adored her little brother. She'd never resent his success. His abilities were so different from hers. But I kept second-guessing myself. Maybe I wasn't seeing everything straight? Maybe she really needed extra attention? The doctor seemed pretty sure that this was the root of Addison's trouble.

But Addison began to look sick. She stopped going outside, stopped bathing. She stopped brushing her teeth and hair, she lived in her pajamas. She never slept, either. She'd be up all night sketching this Ida, this specter, whatever you want to call it . . . I took a picture of her and showed it to her, and I asked, "Do you even recognize yourself, sweetheart? Do you see what you're doing to yourself?" I felt so helpless. I couldn't break through to her.

Addison Stone, summer, Dartmouth, Massachusetts, courtesy of Maureen Stone.

Ida was the ghost who controlled Addison's imagination. She was this old-fashioned girl, always in this same dress, a "day dress," I think they used to call them, with a soft tuck and pleat, lacework at the sleeve, and a pendulum necklace. Addison saw her so intensely.

"Please stop drawing that girl," I'd plead. "You've made yourself sick, drawing her."

"Ida *wants* me to draw her." This was always Addison's response. "She wants me to breathe the life back into her."

Of course it wasn't my parents who made me leave. It was when Addison got in her head that Ida hated her artwork.

"Ida doesn't think my pictures have potential."

"Ida says I'm not intelligent. She thinks I'm a copycat."

"Ida says I'm not as talented as she is."

"Ida says I'll die all alone in a white dress in a white room with no windows or doors. Just like her."

So, yes, I believed that Ida was becoming a real threat. I had to call Roy. He'd stayed in Peace Dale for the summer, to give our marriage some "space"—and I knew he'd be angry that we were cutting his alone time short.

"We have to leave Dartmouth," I told him. "Something is unfixing in Addison's brain. It's not right, and I don't like being stuck here in the country, worrying about it."

MADDY MEYERS: My grandparents have lived at 21 Lyn Road for over fifty years. Still, one afternoon, Mom and I sneaked off to the Dartmouth Public Library's records department. Just see if there'd ever been an Ida. All we found was someone named Calliope Saunders. So maybe that was "Miss Cal" or maybe not. We didn't have any proof. And, by the way, proof of what? Of a poltergeist?

Mom and I also found a house plan. Addison was right that the dining room once had been split into a smaller room plus a pantry—but Mom thought she remembered Gran once telling everyone that. Anyway, it seemed obvious to Mom and me that the problems were mostly in Addison's head.

ROY STONE: Maureen left things too long. By the time I said, "Come back home to me," Addison had starved herself. She looked like a prisoner of war, a skeleton in a T-shirt. You want to know something? It was one of the few times I'd been so angry with my wife that I had no words. And when I looked into my daughter's eyes, I knew we'd all failed her. But that wasn't anything compared with what happened the next week.

Maureen and I were both on watch, but *that* morning Maureen was gallivanting off somewhere. Luckily, I was close by. Only down the road. Needed to see a neighbor. At some point, I said, "Something feels wrong," and I hightailed it back home. Don't know how I knew, but I went straight into the bathroom. There she was, in a white sundress, blood in rivers on the bathroom tiles, seeping into the mat.

I picked her up—she couldn't have weighed more than a hundred pounds. I called 911. I got her the ambulance. I acted quick; you can bet that. She was loaded up within five minutes—she'd have died, if they'd been any later. She was bleeding out.

At the hospital when the doctors started talking about psychotic tendencies and hallucinations, I was all, "Come again?" Maureen hadn't told me a word about what really went on at her parents' place. She'd led me to think Addison's imagination had been getting the better of her. Let me tell you, since then, I've researched the hell out of mental illness. Go ahead, you can ask me anything. I got all the answers.

MAUREEN STONE: That morning, I was interviewing for the job I'm at now, a clothing store called Rick-Rack. So yes, I was preoccupied. And Roy, well, he didn't ever want to hear that our daughter was gravely ill in a way that he didn't understand. He'd keep insisting she had a garden-variety eating disorder. Every time I tried explaining to him about the voices—he didn't want to listen. He thought I didn't have enough control over Addison, that I was "soft" on her, that I should have been getting her to eat regular meals. We were in a struggle every time we spoke of Addison. We'd been back from my parents' house for about a week, and fortunately Addison wasn't sketching Ida or any of those other imaginary people. I never let my guard down, but Addison did seem stable. Dr. Tuttnauer had said to watch out if she seemed in a bliss state, but I'd have never called her blissful. Just stable.

So when Roy's text came in, dear Lord in heaven, I didn't believe it. I was . . . shocked is too gentle a word. I got to the hospital just after they'd pumped her stomach. She was so tiny in that white hospital bed. The gauze wrapping was thick as oven mitts. Here was a girl who'd never been sick, never got colds or croup or flus or fevers. Now Charlie was another story; he was sick all the time, ear infections, summer virus, oh, you name it, we were always rushing him to the doctor's. Never Addison.

I sat by her bed until she woke up. And then my daughter turned her head and stared at me with her big, sad, dark eyes, and she smiled. She told me that Ida had followed her from Dartmouth.

"I guess Ida'll find me if she wants, Mom."

It just about broke my heart.

DOMINICK LUTZ: To talk about Ida, first I should explain I got to be friends with Addison only after she'd moved from Rhode Island to New York City. That night—it was sometime in early fall, I think—my brother and I had arranged to meet Addison at Lucey's Lounge in Gowanus. Lucey's is this dive bar where you get a bucket of ponies, a bucket of popcorn, and sit in the back for six hours, and nobody'll bother you. A lot of artists hang out there. It's a solid scene.

As one half of the Lutz brothers, my twin brother

Cameron—Cam—and I are artists. We're known for being off the radar—just try to find a public image of us; you can't—and working huge. We put twelve-man crews on some of our outdoor installations, and we use real shit: bronze, wood, marble, mortar.

Just like everyone else on the scene, Cam and I'd been seeing Addison Stone's art hit. We'd seen *Talking Head* and the Fieldbender portraits; we knew this artist was becoming major. But we didn't know much else.

Some people were saying Addison was a South American guy—but that turned out to be another street artist, Arturo Heron, who uses gas and electric light in his work, and who mostly gets the credit for *Stop Thinking (About It)*, just like Addison got credit for some of his stuff. Other rumors had it she was a team of people. But then someone tipped us off: this was an American girl, too young to be that good, but the real deal. Everyone wanted to meet her.

That night, I arrive at Lucey's, and in the back room already are my brother, Cam; his girlfriend, Paloma; and Zach Frat, who was Addison's tool of a first boyfriend. And then I saw her. I was blown away, totally. This ghost-goth-punk-heartbreak girl. Black witch hair and hollow black eyes and when the light caught them, thin, pale-ridged scars up her wrists.

At first, it was all of us drinking quietly while Paloma was mouthing off. Paloma's a sweetheart, but she's got too many opinions, and she never comes up for air. I kept squinting at those scars down Addison's arms.

"Bad day at the office?" I finally asked, pointing at them. I wasn't letting the elephant leave the room. I needed the story.

She smiled. Addison's smile was one of those ear-to-ear visual ka-bangs. Lit up her whole face, turned her from Miss Gorgeous into Miss Mischief.

"Don't worry," she said, "I don't listen to everything Ida says. I only let her visit if she can bring us the right synchronicity."

And then, like the way somebody else might describe a walk in the rain, she started telling me about Ida, who was also an artist, who lived up in Massachusetts, who one summer started following Addison around and wouldn't leave her alone.

"Ida was hoping to study at the Sorbonne. She showed me how to draw portraits, how to use oils."

"So you should let her visit you here in New York," I said.

"Oh, no." Addison started laughing, shaking her head. Like I was the crazy one. "Ida died of pneumonia a hundred years ago. That's why she and I cut my wrists. She gets in these black moods, especially when she sees me doing everything she wanted to do. But I've got the best of her in me—look, look how she helps."

Sketch of Ida by Addison Stone, courtesy of Dominick Lutz.

Next thing, Addison whips out a ballpoint, and in this very focused, almost trance-like way, she sketches Ida on a placemat. It was a great sketch: a wistful, sad, pretty girl in a downcast three-quarter profile, with her fingers holding a locket that's on a chain around her neck—technically a difficult angle to draw, especially in a gloomy bar, with a ballpoint, on a placemat. Afterward, I took the drawing and slipped it inside a notebook in my backpack.

From that night on, I believed what Addison told me. It made sense, if you could take that leap—that Addison's talent was touched by something extra, maybe even something otherworldly? Or at least I could believe in her absolute faith that this was true. Which makes it true, in a way, right?

DR. EVELYN TUTTNAUER: I was scheduled to see Addison in a week, after her return from her grandparents' house. Three days before her suicide attempt, we'd exchanged a video call, perhaps forty minutes long. I was concerned about the hallucinations, but they'd stopped completely since she'd returned home. I spoke with her mother, who promised to look for any shifts in behavior.

So yes, I was shocked that Addison Stone had attempted to kill herself. This was no cry for help, either. Lacerations to both wrists, plus a dozen two-milligram tablets of diazepam. Often when the attempt is halfhearted, the lacerations are light and crossways. Addison's wounds went deeper. Up and down. That young woman really wanted to leave this world. In every subsequent visit, when we spoke about the suicide, she never faltered, telling me that Ida had suggested it, and that they'd done it together, and that she hadn't been afraid.

LUCY LIM: The minute I came back from Lake George, my mom sat me down and dumped it on me. That Addy'd swallowed pills and slit her wrists with razor blades. I'd hardly heard from Addy that summer—at first, she'd sent me fun snail mail, these teeny works of perfect postcard art, sketches and jokes and watercolors. But then she seemed to lose interest in all that. And she was never much for being online, but by mid-July her texts had totally dried up. She didn't do

Facebook either, so I couldn't check in with her that way. She was like a balloon that had disappeared up into the sky.

The worst part of Mom's news was, for a split second, how damn glad I felt. Addy hadn't been writing me, but not because she didn't want to be friends with me. Because she'd been going completely insane. Well, praise the Lord and pass the potato salad.

Then panic set in. Oh my God, no! Addy would rather be without me than with me? She would have left the planet, she would have slipped into death without a good-bye?! I told Mom I'd start a hunger strike if she didn't get me a visit to Glencoe ASAP.

So I was the first non-family member to see Addy in the loony bin. I remember I'd dressed up, in heels and a purse—what do you wear to visit your friend who's been committed? I'd brought a homemade lemon angel food cake, since it was her seventeenth birthday that week. They took me to a rec room, where she was sitting in the corner playing Wii with some homeless-looking dude. I recognized her pajamas as the same ones she'd worn at my seventh-grade birthday sleepover, which made me sad—puffy little clouds, too short at the wrists, so the bandages appeared extra-conspicuous. When Addy saw the cake, I could tell she'd forgotten all about her birthday. She looked about nine years old, and she also looked ninety. It was shocking to see her like that.

"Why'd you do it, Addy?" I asked her.

She thought about that.

"I wanted to get to the end," she answered. "I wanted to see what Ida saw. She told me I wouldn't be alone, because she was waiting for me. 'Come home,' she'd tell me. Over and over. At some point, it sounded like a good idea."

"Weren't you scared?" I asked.

"No. I wasn't scared. In that moment, I was finished with life. I wanted something else. I can't explain it to you more than that."

I held back my crying till I got to the parking lot. Addy had become a shadow of the friend I loved.

"She's going to live in that ugly hospital with all those other sad, shadow people forever," I told my mom. "She doesn't care enough to want to get out." Then I went and looked through every Bristol and Dartmouth public record I could get my hands on, searching to see if I could find this monster, this demon, Ida. But at that time, I found nothing.

I'd sold Addy short. By mid-September, she'd bounced right outta Glencoe. Except for those scars, it was like it never happened. She was seeing her doctor every other day, but otherwise, she was like any normal girl. She had a full course load, she was focused, and she looked good, too, she really did! Not like some sick, crazy girl. Always in her leggings and long-sleeved shirts, and she'd painted her tired old last-year's boots this shiny pop of silver-grey, and they were killer. Addy always could turn twenty bucks into two hundred, style-wise.

Most of the kids at South Kingstown had no idea what a private, violent hell her summer had been. She kept that side of herself secret; she was so ashamed of it.

Her first day back reminded me of this other time in eighth grade, when Addy decided to DIY-ink herself with India ink and sewing needles. She came to school with a purple-black rose tattoo above her knee. It was a screwup, and it looked like a mean bruise, but she never mentioned it. Just like the tattoo, her wrists became another thing that we never talked about.

CHARLIE STONE: My sister got discharged from Glencoe after five weeks. I knew she'd had electroshock, and I knew her meds were the reason why she slept all the time, even more than usual, and why there was no snap in her bones. The day Mom drove her home, her scars were so raw I wouldn't look. She seemed unplugged. Drugged and floppy, a rag doll.

That same summer, I'd grown three inches and had been in the sun playing sports all day, making friends, doing fun shit, and having a ball.

"How was your summer?" she asked me first thing.

"Best summer of my life. And you?" I asked.

She laughed. Addison liked dark jokes. "Yeah, same," she said. And then we both kind of cracked up, and I gave her a hug, but underneath the joking, shit, I felt really bad for her.

DR. EVELYN TUTTNAUER: Addison was in my care all that next year. In her regular therapy sessions with me, she revealed a tendency toward depression, punctuated with manic episodes where she produced a great deal of artwork. There were additional but rare hallucinatory incidents, for which I'd prescribed the anti-psychotic Zyprexa. She always called it Z.

While Addison had self-destructive impulses, I wouldn't say she was ruled by them. When she was stable, I'd have described her as an ambitious, energetic, dramatic, and passionate young woman. Very giving, too: of advice, of her time, of actual gifts. She'd once taken off her own scarf and wrapped it around my neck and said, "Keep it, Doc. You look great in lilac." When she felt good, she wanted others to feel good. She was nurturing. Ironically, she preferred the role of therapist to patient.

When Addison moved to New York, my colleague Roland Jones, who is an attending at Weill Cornell, began to see her three times a week. In-person visits trump phone-ins, always. You can learn a lot more about a patient by eyeballing them.

And when it came to discussing Addison's case, Roland and I were in a constant feedback loop. She was in both of our care.

LUCY LIM: Look, my parents have split custody of me. Split custody can be a crap sandwich, but the 'rents try to make it work. Addy's family was the opposite—semi-okay on the surface, but uncover the lid, and it's a boil-over of resentment between two people who shouldn't even be sitting in the same room together, let alone married.

It was me and Mom who cared for Addison after Glencoe. She didn't want to go back home. At my house, she had her own room, food in the fridge, peace and quiet. In the beginning, Addy's doctors were trying her out on different levels of Z, turning up and down the knobs and dials of her brain, which she said made her feel like a human guinea pig. So she was pretty out of it, tired, overwhelmed, distant, and she took these long naps—usually conked out on my bed.

At first, Addy post-attempt-and-new-on-Z was an adjustment. Those scars were downright freaky. She was always the girl in the long sleeves on a hot day. The girl staring out the window, the girl a little spaced and not raising her hand. But eventually, she evened out, and her art began kicking some serious ass.

Addison taking one of her many naps in Lucy Lim's bed, courtesy of Lucy Lim.

Our SKpades *Student* "Spotlight ON" *interview this week
is spotlighting Addison Stone!
Everyone knows Addison, a
long drink of a junior who has
been taking over a lot of the art
room this year. We caught up
with her at Fieldbender Central
to get the scoop.*

Detail from *Cave of Faces* by Addison Stone.

SKpades: Addison, talk to *SKpades*
about your personal style.

Addison Stone: Apathetic?

SKpades: Ha. That's untrue! You
bring it. Examps, people love your
T-shirts. You should sell them. Have
you ever wanted to get into the fashion industry?

AS: Designing clothes isn't my thing anymore.

SKpades: Ooookay, then explain this ginormzee painting? Everyone is
talking about it.

AS: *Cave of Faces.* I didn't know it would grow so big.

SKpades: Yeah, last week when they put it up in front of the
auditorium, everyone was like, "Errrmerrgaahhd! Whoa! It
must be, like, twelve feet high!"

AS: Yeah, I love it. From down the hall, it looks organic, right? Like
something from nature. Then as you come closer, your eyes pick out
those faces, which makes it more interactive. Not natural, but social.

SKpades: Wow, that is so true! My brain just exploded! Last question—
tell us what you did on your summer vacation.

AS: I went to see my grandparents. Oh, and my brain also exploded.

LUCY LIM: After Glencoe, Addy quit all her other hobbies. No more theater, no more dance class, no more local modeling for department stores. Even when she came over to my house to watch a movie, she'd be buried in her sketchbook. Her art was showing up everywhere. She did the cover of the yearbook, the *Our Town* play program. Pretty much anything that the school needed, art-wise, Addy was happy to do.

That fall, it was like Addy singlehandedly rebranded South Kingstown as an art school. It gave her a lot of pleasure to walk down the school halls and see her paintings up there. She was also working so hard to stay sane. She hated her meds, but they focused her. And of course, they kept Ida away.

Our Town theater program, courtesy of South Kingstown High School.

ADDISON STONE: (from a last recorded interview with ARTYOUNITE.com): I've had a complicated relationship with my meds ever since high school, when I started them. I know Z throws off the switch of the monster-go-round of my own thoughts, so that my life makes sense to me.

But Z sucks. When I'm off it, I feel so free in my skin. Ropes loosen around my brain. I'm sprung. I've got clarity like a rock climber on the summit at daybreak. Everything's in perfect focus. Then the focus becomes *too* perfect, *too* clear, sharp as icicles. (*pause*) I start to lose my toehold, but still I'm trying to hold on for as long as I can. I never want to ask for the ropes to be retied. So it pretty much has to be an act of capture.

Peace Dale Ladies by Addison Stone, courtesy of Nancy Hurley.

IV.
ART ROOM FABLE

JONAH LENOX: I'd seen her, of course. Her art had hijacked South Kingstown. Addison Stone on all the walls. But I met Addison for real her junior year, which was my senior year. Thing is, I feel like I'd always known about her. Like, I knew she'd had these mental issues. Her reputation preceded her by a mile. I'd heard the stories, too. Mostly third- and fourth-hand information.

"You hear she got electric shock for five weeks in the nut-house?"

"You see how her wrists are all scarred up?"

"Does she look crazy to you?"

That's what a lot of kids would say to each other. Did she look crazy? Because she didn't look crazy at all. She was the awesome, cute opposite of crazy.

I'd also seen that clip, the Musketeer girl swinging in the Newport mansion. She never got credit for it back then. But everyone knew. I must have watched that clip a billion times. I was so goddamn ready to meet Addison Stone.

LUCY LIM: True love was not Jonah, a.k.a. The Lenox. True love was Lincoln Reed. Infatuation was Zach Frat. But before Zach, before Lincoln, there was darling Jonah. He and Addy were like two pirates taking down the same ship, or two people stuck on the same broken elevator. They were together because of geography and timing. They both were desperate to be other places and live other lives. As soon as they could get out, they did—Addison to New York and The Lenox to Colorado. But for one year, they were misfits together.

JONAH LENOX: How'd I meet her, as in, how'd it start? So I'll tell you a secret: going after Addison Stone was one of the hardest things I ever did. Maybe because I was so shy about getting served her rejection. Anyway. All week, my friends had been bugging me. A senior who was shy about a junior—Jay-zus. Also I had to end things with this other girl, and I wanted to give that a couple of weeks. Deal with the fallout. It was the longest two weeks of my life.

Finally, I picked my day. Friday, after school. Addison was alone in the art room as usual, with her music cranked, one of her bands that she loved, I think it was Tricky, and the song was "Overcome" on a loop. Addison could get drunk on music. She was stretching a canvas for one of her Fieldbender studies, the art that would make her famous. She said she liked to draw Fieldbender because he was always busy around the art room. "He's live in the wild," as she put it.

I stood in the doorway and watched her for a while. Those ribbed leggings, the long sweatshirts, the chipped, dark nail polish. She was always layered and loose, as close to pajamas as she could get. And long sleeves hid the scars. Addison saw her scars as weakness, a shout-out reminder that her brain had steered her off the cliff. So she hid them.

Addison in the South Kingstown High School lounge, courtesy of Jonah Lenox.

Finally I asked if she needed any help. She waited. Letting me sweat. Then she asked, "Is your company help?"

Ha. I hadn't expected that. I said, "Yeah, maybe," and then I ripped the canvas linen with her, stretched and nailed it to the frame, and of course we got talking. She knew my grandma Sugarfoot, who drove her school bus for a while and who once made Addison spit out her gum into her hand. And we talked about *Macbeth*, which she'd read when she was at Glencoe. It was her favorite play. She could quote a lot of it, like, "Whence is that knocking? How is't with me, whence every noise appals me?" She said she related to Macbeth's meltdown, the way he was spiraling into an abyss even as he kept pushing forward.

She was also straight about Glencoe. She didn't act sensitive. At some point, I went out to the vending machine and got us a Coke to split. We cracked it open and sat, backs against the wall, pouring it all out to each other—music, art, gaming, poetry, politics, comedy, graphic novels, God, goth. You name it. Fuck, I was so electrified by her. I couldn't even think what I'd have done next if Addison hadn't wanted to go out with me, after that first Friday afternoon.

LUANNE DENGLER: You want proof Addison Stone hated me? She broke up me and my boyfriend, Jonah Lenox. He was mine, and she stole him. In fact, it's a great example of the kind of girl she was. If she'd lived, she'd have been that stab-in-the-back bitch who'd try to screw your husband in the bathroom at your own birthday party.

Jonah was the boy trophy of our school. Everyone wanted Jonah. His hotness wasn't the same hot as Addison's brother, Charlie, who's a superjock. Jonah's different. He's got a past—his dad's a drifter, and his mom died a long time ago, so he's practically an orphan. Plus Jonah's an outsider. He was raised on a farm in Cumberland by his grandma, who's part Narragansett Indian and rough as a rhino, even though she's always dressed like she's going to Atlantic City in her triple-string fake pearls. She always wore heels and had a cig hanging out of her mouth while she drove the bus. But if you ratted her out for smoking, she'd make you sit right up behind her. So nobody told.

Sometimes I thought Jonah was nuts for Addison because she was the same lawless as Sugarfoot. It was hard for me to compete with that.

Jonah didn't care about sports except for snowboarding. That's partly why he's out in Colorado now. Most girls keep tabs on their exes, right? I always will on Jonah. His eyes are the color of Jim Beam, and he's got those broad shoulders, and at school you could hear him coming from a mile in those size thirteen shit-kicker boots. I know I'm rambling about Jonah . . . I wish I could have put the same spell on him that Addison did. Instead she used him like a winter coat. Useful till the day he wasn't. All she cared about was herself. Addison Stone was in love with Addison Stone. I'm sure all these interviews are making that crystal clear.

DREW MACSHERRY: Jonah's been my pal since we were ten. His grandma's farm is across from MacSherry Dairy, my family's farm. Jonah's dad took off when he was little. Then one day he returned out of nowhere, and Sugarfoot got out her rifle and ordered him off, and she shot the sky. Everyone talked about that for years. In eighth grade, me and Jonah formed a band, "Shoot the Sky," with my kid brother, Mac, on drums, me on vocals, and Jonah playing lead guitar.

We'd practice out in Jonah's barn. We stank, but we were loud and free. Then one day who's in the barn but this pantherish girl, sitting up on the seat of the broken tractor, sketching us.

"Don't mind me," she said. "I'm here with The Lenox."

She was a gypsy. But Jonah said she was just someone from school. Like Mac, I'm homeschooled, so I didn't know anything about her. But then she was there the next day, and the next, and by the next week Addison had put up an easel, and she'd taken over a corner of the barn. She told me she sold her paintings to the school. I thought she was taking the piss outta me. Who'd have the balls to do that? I always liked that idea, though, of a principal writing checks to a student.

Me and Mac kinda fell in love with Addison—it got to be that on afternoons when she didn't show, we didn't even feel like practicing.

Maggie Lenox Playing Dress-up by Addison Stone, courtesy of the estate of Addison Stone.

JONAH LENOX: Sometimes Addison didn't like to be around her mom, and she hardly ever liked to be around her dad. Roy was a wimp who liked to drink, and then he'd get a head full of steam, and he'd pick on Addison's mom or switch off the music or the TV and shove open the window, even if it was blasting cold out.

"Damn sauna in here," he'd say while we all shivered. "Fresh air's good for your health! TV rots your brain! You'll thank me for it."

So yeah, sometimes Addison came over and slept in our barn. Right in the hayloft, unless Sugarfoot knew she was around, and then she'd coax Addison inside like a stray cat and get her to eat a home-cooked lasagna.

Addison once gave me a painting she did of me, with Sugarfoot hovering in the back, and it was just exactly the right vibe. Me and my grandma didn't talk much, but she was always there, and we were family, real and deep. Sugarfoot had my back. The picture's at Waverly Heights Senior Home now, in her room, right over her bed.

In the House of The Lenox by Addison Stone, courtesy of Ruth Lenox.

ARLENE FIELDBENDER: As co-heads of the South Kingstown High School art department, my husband, Bill, and I had known of Addison Stone since she was Allison back in middle school. Even by that time, she had won a number of local art contests. So when the annual W.W. Sadtler contest was announced, we saw it as a key opportunity for her. William Wentworth Sadtler was a New England businessman who made his fortune in tin and lived most of his life in his wife's hometown in East Warwick, Rhode Island. You see his name a lot on plaques around here, in hospitals and parks.

Sadtler collected many beautiful paintings in his lifetime, mostly portraits, and his foundation had created an annual twenty-thousand-dollar grant for a high school junior or senior in pursuit of an education in art. It's a windfall, and Bill and I have witnessed it as a truly life-changing experience for a student. Not just the money, which is incredible, but just as a way to affirm a young talent. RISD students, Providence College of Art students all submit. It's the brass ring.

So I said to Addison, "Create a portrait, and this money will be yours."

"How do you know?"

"Because, my dear, you are that good."

BILL FIELDBENDER: Addison picked me as her subject. She was making studies of me all that winter. Pencil, charcoal, pen-and-inks. I didn't mind; why would I? I was her most available model. Chances were high that if Addison was in the art room, I'd be there, too. That winter, I was also using the school art room to work on some of my own projects. I'm a dabbler.

"Okay, Bill," she'd say—she never called me Mr. Field-bender—"you're gonna need to sit down for two or three

Billfold/#1 by Addison Stone, courtesy of the estate of Addison Stone.

minutes and let me create exactly the perfect shadow to capture how your neck bags like a baby elephant."

"You sure know how to make your teacher feel handsome," I'd tease.

But I always gave her the time she needed. She never stopped surprising me. Even her early studies were evidence of her extraordinary talent.

ARLENE FIELDBENDER: As soon as Addison committed to a canvas and began to apply the oils for the work that would become *Billfold/#1*, the first of that series, we knew. We just knew. She'd hit another level. On a personal note, I was glad she'd chosen to paint Bill. He was as good to her as a father, certainly better than her own. Sure, there was maybe a touch of hero worship there, but it was harmless. Sweet, even. Addison also really knew Bill. She "got" him—his solitude and curiosity and intelligence. His soul, even. Addison's portraits work psychologically because she wanted to understand the inside of personality every bit as much as she could.

Addison gave the Sadtler submission her all, but she did make a slight joke out of the contest and its hype. In the end, she painted an ornamental gold frame around *Billfold/#1*. As if presenting her entry as a gift.

Once she'd turned in the Sadtler submission, she began

Don't Even Think (About It). She planted two "trees" made out of bent wire and wash buckets, and then she strung a web of threads and thin cords and tiny blinking Christmas-tree lights between them. The branches of the Contest Tree were taped with hundreds of fluttering Monopoly money bills. The Addison Tree was knotted in a snarl of shoelaces and frayed purple ribbons, and she'd used a pocketknife to nick into the wire, creating them to look just like her wrist scars.

When we asked her about the work, Addison said, "I don't want to think about that money, but it's consuming me. I keep imagining lines and cords and lights looping from me to the Sadtler grant and back again. So if I don't win, I guess I'll just turn off the lights."

While Addison is known for her portraits, she captured my heart with that installation. What an interesting, quirky way to capture a mood. That's the moment I recognized that, win or lose, Bill and I needed to do something more by Addison.

I contacted her mother. I said, "Your daughter should be auditing weekend classes at the Rhode Island College of the Arts. I've shown a professor friend of mine some of Addison's work, and he'll let her attend for free."

As you might have learned, Maureen Stone has a hard time with decisions. She gave me the whole song-and-dance: "Gracious, we're only a one-car family, and I'm much too busy to drive Addison! Besides, I don't want her getting that serious about art! And why would she attend college before she's in college?"

In the end, it was Jonah Lenox who drove Addison to Saturday morning art classes at RICA. It was over an hour away from his farm to her house to the campus. Then he had to hang out there so he could take her back home. But Jonah Lenox, luckily, was one of the few people taking Addison's genius seriously.

LUCY LIM: The Lenox had this dooky-green Chevy Impala, and baby, we loved it! He always let me third-wheel it with him and Addy. I'd been scared of him when he was going out with Luanne Dengler. But he was so sweet to me. Soon I forgot that he'd been anything but Addison's guy. The three of us would jump in his car and have these adventures. "Let's go to the beach! Let's go to the Wakefield Mall for Friendly's Fribbles! Let's go to the Mystic Aquarium and watch the dolphins!" Didn't matter what. We'd drive around and sing that old Beastie Boys' song about how we holla in a Chevy Impala.

I didn't always come along. But I always felt invited. Those were some of my best afternoons, the three of us lurching down Route 114 in that car, looking for something to do.

MAUREEN STONE: Jonah was a good boy. I'd never have prevented Addison from seeing him. He was a diamond in the rough. After that summer she'd had, goodness, I was happy to see her that way. She was quite secretive whenever Jonah called. She'd giggle and run up to her room with her cell phone. When she was with Jonah, she acted, well, normal, I suppose? Like any teenager.

DUSTIN GERAHY: I was the only other junior taking Advanced Placement art at South Kingstown High School. Me and Addison Frickin' Stone. She was incredible. An art-room fable, a story to tell my grandchildren.

It's not like I sucked—I'm at Carnegie Mellon now, majoring in graphic design. But art class with Addison was like being thrown into a baseball game with the pitcher for the Red Sox. I was cut down to size before I had a chance to prove a thing. Addison was a whole other league of talent.

The other art students knew it, the Fieldbenders knew it. The art room was Addison's fiefdom, and her projects, like those *Billfold* paintings, they were our kingdom's treasures.

My first love? I'll never tell! But I remember my first kiss. It was in a barn, on a working farm way out near Cumberland. The kisser was Jonah Lenox, "The Lenox" I liked to call him, like he was a rare, wonderful species of something. He lived on that farm, and sometimes I lived there, too, when I couldn't deal with the circus clown car of my home life.

Kiss night was black as pitch. We were in rolling around in the hay. With tongue and a hand on the boob— what bee-sting I've got. The Lenox had square, warm hands. I opened my eyes in the middle of the kiss. It's

the curse of an artist, right? To want to observe and record while experiencing?

It was too dark to see, and I was grateful for that. It would have been an overly visual experience otherwise. In the dark, I could concentrate on tongues, mmm, synesthesia. Like being deep under the blue-green water at Point Judith beach. Or sleeping under the warm sun with my toes pedaled in the sand. The Lenox was delectable. Sweetest guy I ever met. He loved my art, too. An early true believer. That was a big deal for me.

Billfold #2/Billfold #3 portraits of Bill Fieldbender by Addison Stone.

ARLENE FIELDBENDER: We did feel like her parents. Perhaps we crossed some boundaries. If we knew she was coming into the art room to work before class, Bill and I'd bring in coffee and breakfast biscuits, and then over breakfast, we'd talk to her about balancing art and schooling. We didn't want to pressure her about scholarships and art schools and competitions. At the same time, we knew she could win them all. It was so tantalizing for Bill and me, just to think of the bigger world recognizing and celebrating her talent.

When Bill and I had lived in New York, a zillion years ago as students at Hunter College, we found such a supportive community. It was only once we'd launched her that we realized Addison had no network in New York, not the way Bill and I had. I will always wrestle with it. Could we have prevented it? Did we encourage bad decisions in her life, because we believed too hard in the good of her talent?

That squid she ended up signing her life away to, Max Berger, could very likely buy a small country off all the money he's made from the Addison Stone domain. The selling of a dead young supernova. Despicable. The other day, I saw someone wearing a T-shirt with Addison's face on it. Max Berger must have licensed that. He's a revolting opportunist. Bill and I never would have thought this would be lovely Addison's legacy. When we knew her, we were blinded by her potential. In love with it, I suppose.

DUSTIN GERAHY: You know, as brilliant as Addison was, people also wanted to sabatoge her. "Tall poppy syndrome," they call it in Australia. Meaning if Addison was the brightest, most beautiful flower standing in the drab field of South Kingstown High School, first we wanted to stare up at her, and then we wanted to cut her down. A lot of kids joked that she didn't have a real home. That she slept in the art room like a ghoul, sucking on the oil paints for nourishment. I'd joke, too. Addison was beautiful, but she also looked like a girl who'd just woken up from an all-nighter in a broom closet.

EVE LIM: Roy's drinking was becoming an issue, a small-town scandal. There was a rumor he was having a fling with a local girl, Shona Barrett, whose parents own Shona's—a sandwich shop over on Greenhill Beach. Lucy would go to Addison's house and then report that Shona'd been there making eyes at Roy, both of 'em drinking cheap box wine with pop radio blasting, while Charlie was off at sports practice and Maureen was walled up in her bedroom, watching television. No wonder Addison didn't want to be there.

BILL FIELDBENDER: I was passing through the school's faculty lounge one evening—I'd been at a policy meeting till late, and I found Addison curled up in an armchair, sketching and eating a bag of Doritos. "Hey, Bill, tonight I'm sleeping here," she explained, "because my folks had a fight." Very matter-of-fact. As if sleeping inside her high school was a reasonable option. That was when my brain pulled the fire alarm.

That next morning I emailed the high school summer program at Pratt Institute. I wanted Addison capital O-U-T out of Peace Dale. Sadtler money or not, we could rescue her through a summer program. She'd be turning eighteen, and Arlene and I reckoned she could even stay in New York through the next school year. Then she could start laying down a solid groundwork of classical knowledge, as well as focusing her training on form and technique, and make up any additional required classes at the Professional Children's School—a highly accredited school that is specifically for young people in the arts.

Look, my wife and I are small Rhode Island potatoes, but we're on good terms with plenty of well-connected people in the New York art scene. We thought they could be her sponsors and her mentors. We saw invitations and opportunities well beyond what anyone here could give her. We didn't see issues. Not the way we should have. That's how badly we wanted Addison out of Peace Dale. That's how badly we wanted her to soar.

LUCY LIM: The Fieldbenders were fricking bananas to get Addy out of Peace Dale. They pushed it hard. They'd even plan these little "spontaneous" meet-ups with me and The Lenox, because they wanted us to whisper in Addy's ear about how she needed to go to New York, how New York was the only place that could "handle her genius." At first, we were all like, "Enough with your crazy!" I mean, Addy was too young to pack up and leave home. She wasn't even eighteen till summer!

Besides, Addy said her own mom was a big obstacle to the Fieldbender plan. Addy cracked us up, imitating her mom wringing her hands and whimpering, "Oh goodness gracious, oh dear, oh dear. Over my dead body will I let my daughter get eaten by wolves in New York!"

And then, just when we thought the argument was over and the Fieldbenders had dropped it, Addy won that W.W. Sadtler thing, *plus* her *Talking Head* painting of Mrs. Hurley won the Maynard Prize. Everything changed. The newspapers were all over it. They did a huge article on her in *Parade* magazine, and another one in *The Narragansett Times*, and then it seemed like she didn't belong anywhere *but* New York City. So it all got settled pretty quick, zip-zilch-zot.

BILL FIELDBENDER: "Your Future Goes Here" is sponsored by the Maynard Institute. It's a privately funded program that gives away about five million dollars a year to students by way of grants and prizes. Arlene and I had submitted Addison's painting of Nancy Hurley, who is South Kingstown's school principal.

Nancy has been our school principal for almost twenty years, so she's a well-known face in these halls. Everyone loves Nancy; she's an institution. What I love most about the painting Addison did of her is that it shows Nancy in a different light. Not the jolly, smiling, lively lady we all recognized. There's something quiet and unguarded and intimate about it; you feel like you're kind of creeping up on Nancy while she's asleep. In a final touch, Addison etched *MOM* above her head, which is definitely the way many students think about Nancy.

ARLENE FIELDBENDER: Of course it wasn't lost on any of us that both Bill and Nancy were, in a sense, stand-in parent figures. Addison only painted people she felt emotionally connected to. But *Talking Head* was interesting, too, because it had the technical chops that the Maynard appreciates. Addison tended to work large. Lots of thick paint applied to giant canvases. She'd started the piece mid-December and worked straight through the holiday break—we even gave her keys so she could come in when the school was locked up.

BILL FIELDBENDER: Arlene and I submitted it ourselves because we knew Addison wouldn't have bothered with the mundane paperwork details. We'd hoped that she could get some recognition from real institutions. Every single thing Addison was doing deserved recognition—and nobody in her inner circle seemed to care. Well. I cared. My wife cared.

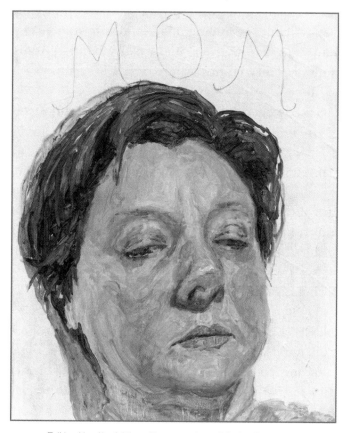

Talking Head by Addison Stone, courtesy of Carine Fratepietro.

MAUREEN STONE: Addison came home one day in late spring and said, "Mom! I won twenty grand from the W.W. Sadtler Foundation and five thousand from the Maynard Institute. No strings attached. So I guess I'll be going to New York after all."

Twenty-five thousand dollars! Merciful heaven, I just didn't know what to say. Roy's and my jaws dropped. Our fight to stop Addison from running off to New York City just crumbled away—how could we hold up an argument against it?

Of course, Arlene and Bill Fieldbender had to play queen and king of the chessboard. The way they smiled at me and Roy, with daggers in their eyes. "No need to worry. We've taken care of everything."

Over and over. No matter what I said, one or the other would answer, "We already thought about that" and "Everything is paid for" and "One of us will see to that." They'd found Addison a dorm and a chaperone. They even called Addison's psychiatrist, Dr. Tuttnauer, and helped her to secure Addison a new psychiatrist, Roland Jones, in the city. The Fieldbenders ladled poison in Dr. Tuttnauer's ear, I'm sure, about how Addison had to get away from her small-minded family and her smaller-minded town.

When we all sat down together, I could feel their resistance to everything Roy and I said or thought. They believed we couldn't provide anything for Addison. Their judgment flavored every word out of their mouths. Heaven knows, I never wanted to hold Addison back. But she'd been so sick, and junior year, she'd been doing so much better. I didn't want her to lose that.

Whatever else these interviews are telling you, about our family, our struggles, and Addison's desire to be free of us, I promise, it was never, ever as bad as you'll hear. Blame poverty, blame family—but mostly, blame the mother, right? It's an old story, isn't it? I will tell you, though, if my daughter had stayed in Peace Dale, she'd be alive today. Because I would have been watching Addison. I was always watching her.

But I couldn't watch her once she dropped out of sight.

Addison Stone, summer before senior year, courtesy of Lucy Lim.

V.
"THEY NEED TO LET
ME COME BACK."

ADDISON STONE (clip from the interview "Twenty Under Twenty-Five: New York Artists to Watch"): Every artist remembers her first time seeing New York. I'm no different. My boyfriend drove me down from Rhode Island on the I-95 through the Palisades, the Bronx, Harlem. You get an assload of ugly smack in the eye even before you hit midtown. My body was caffeine, malted milk balls, and adrenaline.

First thing I did was dump my bags at my shoebox dorm room at Pratt, and then I headed straight to Carine Fratepietro's gallery show. Sweaty palms! By then I'd completed three of my *Billfold* series, the paintings I was doing of Bill Fieldbender, plus the one of Nancy Hurley, which had gotten me a lot of attention. My "Mom and Dad" paintings, we called them.

That first day-into-night, I was wearing my Converse All-Stars and drainpipe jeans and a purple T-shirt with paint splattered all over it, but I didn't have time to change. Also, to be honest, I don't care about shit like that. Sure, I'll wear the sparkly gown, especially if it's a freebie. But I do better if I walk into a room as me. Fashion is art, but I'm not someone who needs costumes or flashiness to signal myself. The work itself has to speak loudest.

Irony was, what I wore that night defined my first brush with the press. Everyone ended up writing about Addison Stone—the "Maynard winner" and the "Chandelier Girl" and "hot young artist"—who showed up to her first opening looking like a junkie. Hand to God, I didn't care. I looked bad, but I looked good, you know? I came through the door exactly the way I wanted.

CARINE FRATEPIETRO: I was born in Lyon, France, but now I have homes everywhere. Or maybe my home is on airplanes. My life is hectic. I raised my son Zach in this jet-set lifestyle. Italy one day, Miami the next. When all your passion is art, you are always tracking in search of the next new star. I do believe that my son benefitted from a global education, but some days, I wonder if the whole craziness of Zach and Addison was because he was too used to the game of pursuit.

I was an artist long ago, before I learned that my real gift is my eye. I see what others don't. My private collection was recently valued at two hundred million. I will tell you now, it's worth more—though it is never good for people to know how much money you have. Addison Stone's chandelier video was youth and beauty and laughing in the face of death. Her portrait paintings showed immense knowledge, sensitivity, and sensuality. She was too young for such breadth. I did not believe it. But my eye knew not to look away.

That night of her opening, I had a dinner engagement. It was Zach who met her first. Momentous, yes? Suddenly they were together all the time, the magazines, gossip sites . . . it seemed that all at once, the world revolved around Addison and my son. Zach is a party boy. It's not good to present yourself to the world as a party girl because of the company you keep. But that sword was double-edged, no? Because my son will never shake his fateful connection with Addison Stone.

ZACH FRATEPIETRO: When my mother can't be at openings, she likes me to go for her. She's old-school European, and so she thinks a member of the family should always be present, to act as host. The art world is tiny and powerful, and I have a good eye, too. I'm more serious than the press makes me out to be. My biggest career issue is that the press hates

Zach Frat, New York, courtesy of Alexandre Norton.

society kids. They think we're trust puppies. The press started calling me "Zach Frat" and "Zach Brat" all the way back when I was at Collegiate. But I only party as hard as the next guy.

Alexandre Norton's family has even more money than mine, and they never give him the shit they give me, because Alex doesn't strive to be more than a good-time guy. I'm serious about my future. People don't understand that your last name only gets your foot in the door, which can be a blessing *and* a curse. Being the "son-of" is a pretty limited narrative. And people want you to fail on that; people judge you harder. People assume you get all the breaks. Addison wasn't my easy break—I found her all on my own. I was onto Addison before Carine or any of the gallerinas had her on their radars. I'd seen pictures of Addison. She was so hot. Sometimes Russian looking, other times South American, sometimes Asian or French. I never knew a girl who could look so many different ways. With those glittering eyes and that secret smile.

Talking Head went for a joke price. I think Addison sold it to us for six thousand or something? She wasn't with Max Berger at that point, so my mother bought it outright. Cheap as it was, Addison was still the featured star at the group show my mother was exhibiting through Berger Galleries. They exhibit and sometimes resell our private collection, along with their own pieces.

There were a lot of up-and-comers that night, and I'd handpicked most of the art on the walls. But Addison was my It Girl. She was my discovery.

ARLENE FIELDBENDER: Bill and I set it up. We are both guilty as charged. Can you blame us? It was too easy. We clipped a few photographs of Addison, along with her recent press and a scan of some of her portfolio pieces, and we emailed everything with a note to Zach Fratepietro. We knew her face would catch his attention, and we knew he bought art on behalf of his mother. The ball was rolling so fast and hard with Addison. Getting her into a real New York show was absolutely the next piece of it. I said to Bill, "Zach Fratepietro couldn't spot talent if it bit him on the balls, but he will respond to a pretty face. And then Carine will be able to see what Addison is." Zach will always be under his mother's thumb. At the same time, he'll always be desperate to prove that he "discovered" the next Big Thing.

Of course they bought the piece immediately, because Addison had priced it too low. We thought she could get twenty times that amount, and we encouraged her to sign with a smart dealer, but Addison could be stubborn. Anyway, she now had plenty of money—all the budget she needed to live in New York City. Clothing allowance, food and living expenses, all of it.

Bill and I hadn't counted on the fact that Addison would end up turning over most of that money to her family. We had no idea Addison stayed poor as a church mouse all that first New York summer. We only found out about that much later.

ZACH FRATEPIETRO: Friday night of Addison's first show was insane. I don't know who leaked it. It was the usual gallery opening scene, but it felt jacked up. Everyone seemed to know that Addison was newsworthy. It was like she had this pre-fame. The gallery was wall-to-wall people: the regular money crowd, plus the celebs and the hangers-on in their velvet blazers and stilettos and fake eyelashes and micro-miniskirts, and then Addison, killing it in her jeans and messy hair and paint splotched down the front of her shirt. She was an original.

It takes one-fifth of a second to fall in love. That's what popped into my mind the moment I saw her. It happened that quick for me, too. Quicker, even.

ALEXANDRE NORTON: Zach and I are second cousins. Blood is thicker than water, but we'd have been tight even without our blood connection. We started at Collegiate in pre-K. I know that guy better than I know myself. And I knew, that night, I knew bone-deep that this new girl, this Addison, was trouble. I knew my cousin would be throwing it all away for her. I could feel that he would do that, and she wouldn't be worth it.

And I was right on every count.

LUCY LIM: That night of Addy's exhibit in New York City, I was up visiting my dad on Lake George as usual. Not sure how, but Lake George had, since the last summer, become even worse than watching-paint-dry boring. The only halfway fun part was Addy's first night in the city, how she looped me in and made me be part of it. So fun! My phone was going *zzzp zzzp zzzp* every thirty seconds. Every picture had my eyeballs zinging! The crowd was too beautiful! The art was too strange! I don't get art. But Addy's face was glowing, lit up, and you could tell she didn't want to miss a thing.

Then she Snapchatted me a photo of this guy, Mr. Prep School with the swoopy haircut. He wasn't model-hot, but he was sort of asshole-hot. He was the guy with the best shoes and the quickest, cruelest put-down. In the picture, he was wearing a buttery-yellow summery silk shirt that looked like it cost more than my dad's Sunfish. Next up was a double-selfie where they're both raising wine glasses, and then the next one was the two of them nuzzling, and I was like, *Ahhhhh. Okay. She's feeling this guy.*

But I knew Addy. She was Snapchatting because of The Lenox, and she didn't want any evidence that she was into Haircut while poor, sweet Jonah was waiting for her at her dorm.

She'd told me that she and The Lenox had agreed, since they would be so far apart, that they wouldn't be against seeing other people. But Addy confessed to me later that she hadn't counted on meeting someone new that very first night.

Around midnight, Addy texted: look up Zach Fratepietro! When I did, I found out he was the son of this dragon-lady art gallery diva that I never heard of, and I found all these pictures of him and his pals like Alexandre at clubs and parties and fashion shows. I'd never heard of any of these big-money people or art people, but I was impressed. They were known. They were young and rich and almost famous.

It was only one summer before that Addy had been committed to Glencoe, where I'd visited her in that room with bars on the windows and seen her sitting balled up, her eyes glazed over, telling me she was finished with life. She'd seemed like such a prisoner of the moment. And now here she was in the heart of New York City, at her own gallery opening, becoming a superstar. She'd shot out of her house and literally straight into the arms of New York's most eligible.

JONAH LENOX: After I'd graduated from South Kingstown, the plan was for me to drive Addison to New York City, maybe hang out a few days, and then head west to Boulder. Once Addison knew she was really leaving, and especially when she got some money in the bank from the Sadtler people, she started detaching. Even though we called it "taking some time off from each other," I knew she was closing her chapter on me. She started buying me stuff, just small things—a sweatshirt, a cool cell phone skin—and I knew, even though I never said anything to her, that it was because she felt bad for me. She wanted to put a Band-Aid on it, but she knew I was just another person in this world who was more into her than she was into me.

We packed the Chevy with all her stuff—her paints and easel, her canvases, a mini-microwave, her millions of art books, her winter coats and boots. We said goodbye to everyone. Her mom and her dad and Charlie and Lucy and Lucy's mom all waved from the front door, but once Addison got in the car, she literally never looked back.

"Hey, turn around and wave to your mom," I said.

She just shook her head no. I knew she felt horrible to be leaving her mom, who had her faults, but who didn't have much else happening in her life, especially once Addison was gone. Not that Addison should have been held accountable for that. But still. Hard.

The closer we got to the city, the more Addison started in on this rant. It was like she had to say goodbye by rejecting everything. Nothing was good in Peace Dale. It sucked, the people sucked, the art sucked. She saw herself as having just barely escaped. The Fieldbenders were like her fairy godparents, and I was the nice guy driving the magical pumpkin.

"Can you believe we're both out, Jonah? I'd have died to stay behind in Rhode Island once you'd left."

"Aw, stand down, Addison. You'd have been okay. You'd have made it work. You've got Lucy, Bill and Arlene, and Charlie. You've got your head on straight."

"That's not true," she answered. "I don't have my head on straight. My head's been on crooked for a long time now."

Well, I didn't want to get into it with her. Her crooked head was made up.

Once we got to the city, I decided not to tag along to the art opening. I was dead tired and wanted to sleep. The plan was that Addison'd come back, wake me up, and we'd roll out to a late dinner. She texted only once from the show that she was running late, and when she finally stumbled in at 2 A.M., I could feel my heart rip a little. I knew she'd had a great time, and that she probably hadn't even wanted to come back at all. Even her skin smelled different.

She climbed into bed, cold and sweaty, complaining about bed spins. Addison wasn't a girl who drank ever. Not with the meds she was on. She mumbled that they just kept feeding her cocktails. That every time she put one down, they'd stick another one in her hand, and even one sip from six glasses could lead to a pretty stiff drink.

"I stayed out too late, and you know I'm an amateur. I'm so sorry, Jonah."

She kept on apologizing, even half asleep, which should

have been a sign, but I didn't want to see it. So I was like, "Cool, let's sleep in tomorrow. Pop some popcorn, hang out, talk, maybe take the subway to the Met later on."

We curled up together and crashed, and the next morning, I went on a Starbucks run, and when I come back, who's sitting in the room right on the edge of the same bed where we'd just been sleeping, but this guy. He's pressed and ready in his tassel shoes and knife-cut pants and a signet ring. "Hey there, I'm Zach!" With his shit-eating toothpaste grin.

I think Addison was genuinely surprised that he had tracked her down. It was painful for me, but I tried to be cool with it. Still. It was—bang. No matter how many slurred apologies. The bottom line was I'd been fired and replaced.

After Zach left, we hung out, ate the popcorn, talked, just like we'd planned, but the day was empty. Before I left, Addison gave me this sketch—*The Lenox*. Her last gift.

The Lenox by Addison Stone, courtesy of Jonah Lenox.

"I get it that you don't belong to me," I said to her. "Not that you ever did. But I'm already missing you from my life."

"I know," she answered. That was her answer. Not "I'll miss you, too." Not "Maybe it's not over." Just "I know." Addison never liked to bullshit anyone.

The other day on the beach, I was thinking how we all get old, but Addison stays young and perfect forever. Lucy Lim likes to remind me about all the art that Addison left in the world. Like it's a calling card to remember her by. Lucy's a glass-half-full kind of girl. But I can't help seeing a no-Addison world as half empty. She'll always touch the deepest places of my memory, the places you turn over just to feel that bruise and know that it's gone, she's gone, and none of it's ever coming back.

ERICKSON MCAVENA: Addison Stone was my one true friend in the big bad city, and I was hers. Her boys came and went, but I stayed, along with her beloved Lucy "Lulu" Lim. I'll tell you something: in some ways, I reckon I knew Addison better than Lucy did. I knew bright, shiny, photo-ready, outer-shell Addison, but I also knew soft, fierce, inside-core Addison. And that all added up to a complicated girl.

We met that very first week we got to the city. We were both living on the seventh floor of windowless, mushroom-carpeted Esther Lloyd-Jones Hall, which is part of Pratt's student housing. "Where charm goes to die," my boyfriend, Teddy, joked. Addison had landed at Pratt—and, bigger picture, in New York—with a splash, but I hadn't cottoned onto any of that. I had my own shit; I'd just left home—I guess the technical term is "run away"—to live with Teddy.

So I was holed up illegally in the dorm. My parents had cut off my credit card, and I was far from the comforts of Kentucky. The McAvenas are a "name" in Kentucky—if you ever ate a McAvena ham, bless your stars, you've generously contributed to the local dynasty. I myself haven't touched pork since I was eight. As a gay Democrat vegetarian anti-NRA activist, I'm in opposition to just about every dirty little secret that the McAvena name stands for, no matter the benefits.

And the McAvena name couldn't buy me a two-egg special in New York City. I wasn't supposed to start classes at NYU until that fall. I was in limbo. Look, I ended up patching up all my drama with my folks by September. But that summer, it was drama central.

I was a hothead, squeezed into that hamster-cage dorm room with Teddy, who was equally tense, convinced he was gonna be kicked out of Pratt for illegally housing me. I'd met Teddy the year before at Episcopal, which is a boarding school down in Virginny. Two Southern gay boys meet-cute in photography lab, a pair of Mapplethorpe wannabes. My decision to go to NYU was partway to be close to Teddy. But now we were *too* close, sharing 300 square feet.

So here I was, raging to my friends on the phone all day. Raging at Teddy all night. One morning comes a knock on the door. I open it to find this slinky girl with licorice eyes and black hair in two shiny braids. She gives me a once-over and says, "Hey, loud, spoiled Southern boy pissed with the world, here's a cuppa coffee. Now show me what you're working on. Teddy says when you're not bitching at everyone, you take good pictures."

Addison and Erickson, courtesy of Ted Furlong.

LUCY LIM: Erickson McAvena was Addy's lifeline. She was just starting to date Zach, but Addy unfortunately always expected the worst of Zach. I think because her dad was a womanizer, and she knew Zach was, too. So even while Addy was crushing on Zach, she kept him at a distance. He was up on this pedestal, but it was also a pedestal of suspicion.

"Zach's a playboy," she'd tell me. "He's way over-serviced. He's got a personal tailor in Hong Kong who flies into New York and makes him a dozen new shirts each season. He speaks five languages, Lulu! That's just way too many shirts and languages!" In the beginning, Addy loved being seen with Zach, and with his wingman, Alexandre, and basking in the stir they all caused. I think Zach took equal delight as a co-star in the Zach-and-Addy show. They both fed off it.

Erickson was a big personality, too, but he was calm and strong in the center. I love that guy; we'll always be in touch, we'll always share a bond. The week she met him, Addy wrote me this email, which I printed and saved.

From: **Addison Stone** <addisonstoneart@gmail.com>
Date: Jul 23 at 12:07 PM
Subject: hi / more
To: Lucy Lim <lucygracelim@gmail.com>

Thing is, LL, I can be alone while being with Erickson.
We are togetherness in solitude.

On our long walks through the parks.
Or in a tapas bar. In a bookstore,
I am happy in his unfazed Southern company.
The sweet and sleepy St. Bernard eyes.
The tender stories about his screwed-up parents—who sound just like mine.
How he escaped them—just like me.

But always kept his sunshine—just like I want to.

Scarred but not damaged.

Erickson cooks me his Kentucky home recipes in the crummy Pratt kitchen.

Pecan muffins, succotash, sweet potato pie.

And his pictures. Images that should be sad. Poor old men on the subway and crazy pigeon ladies.

Erickson finds the true, deep kind. The sweetness and the real.

He can't replace you, Lulu.

But he's got your way of making me lean into peace whenever I see red.

Please Help, a photograph by Erickson McAvena.

LUCY LIM: She never got as close to anyone else in the city. Lincoln, off and on. Marie-Claire, sometimes. But Lincoln had a lot of emotional barricades mixed up with his passion, and Marie-Claire could be selfish. Erickson was all heart, all for her, always.

MARIE-CLAIRE BROYARD: I'm a New York born-and-bred daughter of, yes, *that* Broyard family. At this time, I'm not in school. You could say I'm between schools. I was at USC for a semester. *Alas*, I wasn't meant for California. So I'm still living in New York. Enjoying my exalted place in the cosmos, I suppose. But enough about me when here's what you want to hear: my fabulous Addison Stone story.

Now this was Addison's first summer in town, but of course being that it was sweltering July, we were all in Southampton. And one night, we were at my friend Kiki Strawbridge's dinner party. Addison was just that second starting to date my friend Zach, and he was *thrilled* to be introducing her to our clique. Usually when one of the boys dates outside our group, it's just some ditzy fashion-model-slash-actress.

But Addison was becoming a star in her own right. There was a rumor she was being repped by Berger Gallery, and that Jürgen Teller was in discussions for her to do an ad, and that she was going to be one of the poster images for Beats headphones—which turned out to be a rumor—but still!

We were ready to *despise* her. And I was doing my part as Queen Bee. The very first thing I ever asked her was, "Oh, Addison, where in the world did you get your bag?" It was this chintzy Canal Street knockoff. And then I asked her where her family skied. Oh, and a hundred other snotty questions. I can really bring out the claws when I want. I was *pummeling* her. I wanted to chip away her façade until she gave me some reaction we could all make fun of—maybe some swearing, or generally losing her cool and going all white trash on us.

Instead, Addison said, in a perfect imitation of my voice, "Back when I was living at Glencoe, which was a *divine* mental health facility outside Boston, with such *fabulous* food, Marie-Claire, it almost makes you forget you're trying to kill yourself every minute, one of our wellness exercises was to 'savor a pleasurable experience.' And so, *darling*, I am truly going to *savor* this." And she picked up her vichyssoise and poured it like a baptism right over my head.

For the first three seconds, nobody moved. Dead silent. Me, too. Yet I felt *committed* to remaining in place. Letting her savor it! Just as she'd said! Then I started laughing. It really was so funny. Oh, and of course after that, we became furiously good friends. She was just too naughty and refreshing. Same kind of naughty as me.

Later, after we'd gotten close, I learned more about her illness. She let me in on that, I think, because I'm pretty frank about my own mother, who just spent her tenth anniversary at McLean. My poor mother, she's schizoaffective, diagnosed when she was nineteen, and she's been to hell and back with it. Mother's breaks with reality are still terrifying for everyone. Once, when I was a girl, she set her own hands on fire. I didn't see it happen; she was in Gstaad. But still, it happened. I see the welts and scars on her palms every time I visit, and I imagine her putting her fingers in the roaring fireplace and holding them there, watching the flames lick her skin, but too trapped in her disease to snatch them out.

Addison felt very easy speaking to me about her own schizophrenia once I told her about Mother. That same fall, after we became friends, Addison and I once drove up to McLean together, very hush-hush, to have my annual birthday lunch. It had been a lovely day, if rather strange and bittersweet. Mother was terribly foggy. I knew Addison didn't like that, since Addison was always paranoid that the Z made her foggy, too.

But it was so sweet and good of her to go with me. I loved Addison because she took me for who I am, with all my family skeletons. My mother, the schizo. My Uncle Artie, the felon. The time I was kicked out of school for cheating. The time I was kicked out for good, when they found weed in my electronic cigarettes. Addison had plenty of heart, and plenty of room in it for other people's shadows.

Addison and Marie-Claire, September, New York City, courtesy of Zachary Fratepietro.

BILL FIELDBENDER: Arlene and I started visiting New York a bit more that summer, just to peek in on her. We'd gotten her there, so we felt some personal responsibility for her general well-being. But we could tell she didn't need us. Right from the get-go, Addison understood the city. It was like it'd been predestined, inked into her karma. You'd have thought she'd grown up in New York. She was as blasé as a Spence girl. She seemed utterly focused, too, attending art classes, and she'd learned the subway map cold. She even took us over to Williamsburg and Long Island City to catch some exhibits.

We were very concerned that she'd be preyed on by dealers and agents. We warned her to please talk that decision through with us, whenever she decided to seek representation. But we also knew that we couldn't prevent what she did next. Week by week, Addison was shaping herself into her own person.

ZACH FRATEPIETRO: It's outrageous that people would think I was capable of harming Addison Stone. I loved her more than anyone else. But our breakup was bad, and our revenge was some dirty tricks. I'm glad I can remember the good times before it all collapsed between us, when Addison was new in the city, fresh and wide-eyed and in love with me.

I was her first real taste of New York, don't forget. The first person to show her the reservoir in Central Park, the MoMA, the top of the Empire State Building. We ate at all the best places: Bemelmans, The Spotted Pig, Cafe Luxembourg, Raoul's, Il Mulino, The Lion. We walked the High Line, biked over the Brooklyn Bridge, told each other secrets in Strawberry Fields. And there was the public aspect, too, the people I introduced her to—Kiki Smith, Julian Schnabel, Terry Richardson, John Currin and Rachel Feinstein, Cindy Sherman. I was with Addison for some of her major moments. That's what I hold onto. The good stuff.

Zach and Addison attend a dinner party in New York, courtesy of Alistair Chung.

MAXWELL BERGER: Everyone knows Berger Gallery. I've been dealing high-end art since before you were born. I'm based in New York City, and we got satellite offices in Asia and the UK and Paris and Brazil. So I don't give my private line to anyone. In a business like mine, who wants some artist wunderkind calling me up at 3 A.M. to see if I can lend him a thousand bucks to score some grade-A blow, just so he can be awake for the next four nights and days to finish a canvas? Who needs that? Not me. Whoever's got my number, well, I usually ignore them, too.

Zach Frat left me six messages before I called him back. He wanted me to meet this new girl.

I finally call back, I say, "Bring her by the Soho House." I like the Soho House, I like the roof-deck pool and the lobster roll and the girls in their skimpy bikinis. Hey, I don't apologize for that. If I can't get to my place in Sagaponauk, I'm there. Art kids know me there, but they keep a respectful distance. They should. They know how many careers I've made—and broken. And I don't do callbacks. But Zach Frat, he's Carine's kid, and Carine, she's a powerhouse.

Next thing I'm out by the pool, I feel the shadow. I open my eyes, and this girl is standing over me. Blocking my sun, or I'd have thought she was a ghost. Beautiful but not my type. Call me old-fashioned, but I like some meat on a girl.

"I'm Addison," she says. "My art was in your show a few weeks ago. You should know the rest of your gallery was crap."

That's what she said to me. This skinny-ass human candlestick girl. To me, Max Berger. Un-fucking-believable. But she was right. Every other piece, you couldn't sell it in the Dairy Queen today. But I could feel my neck get hot. We both knew she was right on the money.

Let me say this about Addison Stone. She didn't just

make art. She *was* art. Same as Picasso, Glenn Gould, Gertrude Stein. You couldn't untangle her from it. I decided then and there to get her into my talent stable. A small-town girl like that, you want to dazzle her hard and sell it fast. I made a date, wooed her at Per Se with some of my people. I threw Zach some extra business so that he'd talk me up. I pitched that snot-nosed teenager as hard as I ever pitched. But the day she said she'd sign with me, I gave her my warning.

"No stunt art, Addison," I told her. "No swinging from the lights, you got it? You are too rare a talent, and I care about you. From now on, stay focused, working, and strategized. I will be there for you, but you need to grow up and learn quick how to weed out the bullshit and the bad advice. I got no sympathy for kids who can't handle the money or the fame. I got no time for drunks, users, and party people. And I got no sympathy for you flushing your own career down the toilet."

She didn't want to hear that. She wanted to be a free agent and do whatever the fuck she liked. They all do. Luckily, money talks. We struck an agreement, and we'd gone to contract by the end of the month.

CARINE FRATEPIETRO: In the late '90s, Max had been imprisoned on a tax fraud scandal. But his nose had been clean for years. And people are flawed, yes? Was every person we introduced to Addison a sparkling moral character? No. This is a business. Like any business, there are good people and bad people and people in the gray middle. Max Berger is gray, no doubt. But he's also very influential, and once he catches whiff of a talent, he makes a lot of noise. He was the megaphone that Addison Stone needed.

ZACH FRATEPIETRO: Crazy summer. For one thing, Addison and I got together exclusively. I was twenty-two at the time, three and a half years older, but Addison wasn't any virgin. I know you didn't ask me that, but I want to put it out there. This can't be the story of the guy who rooked Addison Stone's virginity. I've got enough shit talked about me. Anyhow, she'd lost it already to Jonah. She told me. So by the time she met me, she knew how to have fun.

Once she said, "Sex is the opposite of art. Sex is stupid and thoughtless and easy. Art is complicated and difficult and important."

But she was wrong. Sex meant something to Addison. I could always feel her needing to learn more and more about me intimately, what we liked and what made us feel good versus what didn't, what was just so-so. There wasn't a thing she wouldn't try. I never had a girl want to learn me as deeply as Addison. We'd hang out in bed, and the whole afternoon would be gone while we got lost in each other. We came together physically. Sure, we'd been raised in different universes. But in terms of sex, we were equals; we were twins. Whenever I had to leave her, I couldn't stop thinking about her. I'd stumble around, my body felt lost and radioactive till the next time I saw her. I dreamed about her and woke up crazy for her, hot for her; it felt like it would burn me up, that was how bad I wanted her all the time.

My first gift to Addison was the key to my apartment in Tribeca. The Pratt dorm was hell. I'd been given a top floor of my luxury building the day I turned twenty-one, and I'd made it into a real home. It had perks that were perfect for Addison. Like every morning, they served complimentary breakfast, and there was a gym on the ninth floor, and a maid service, pickup dry cleaners, all that.

"I love your space," she told me, "but I'd love it more if Erickson could eat breakfast here, too. Teddy's always away, and Erickson's so lonely."

"Sure," I said. I thought she was joking. Turned out she wasn't. Addison and Erickson dragged each other around everywhere. Wherever one went, here came the other. It got on my nerves. Why do girlfriends always come packaged with best friends? I was a better influence for Addison, anyway. Erickson was a functioning derelict, in my opinion. Meantime, I'd hooked her up with my dentist, my psychic, my trainer—anyone who I thought could assist Addison, I stepped forward and paid that bill, no question.

"I need so much, but you give me even more," she told me.

I gave her a lot because I had a lot, and I wanted to help her. It made me feel like we were building something together. And for the first time, my apartment felt like home.

MARIE-CLAIRE BROYARD: Darling, say what they will about how much Zach Frat and Max Berger used Addison—and they did, absolutely, each in his own way—nobody but nobody had ever taken care of that girl the way Zach did. I realized it wasn't healthy. In fact, it could make me squeamish; Zach was so obviously buying her love. But Addison seemed almost like a vagabond. Take her parents, for example—do you know I never even met them, not once? They never called or texted or popped in to check up. They seemed entirely off her grid, except for the fact that I knew she was always sending money to them. That's the main thing I knew about Addison's family—that they were on her gravy train. Her high school art teachers were super sweet and obviously adored Addison, but they couldn't be there for her on a day-to-day basis. And she had this therapist, but therapy isn't a community. Therapy's just about keeping a logbook on your sanity.

So maybe Zach did persuade her into the Berger contract. So what? What if he did? What else was on the table? Who else was watching that girl? And Berger Gallery is a community. Everyone who worked there, from the assistants to the buyers, were wild for Addison. Max is slimy, but in the end, he'll guard Addison's legacy like a pit bull for the rest of his life. Ultimately, all Berger cares about is making sure that valuable art stays valuable.

ROY STONE: So you want to ask me about Max Berger's contract? Fine. Yes. Maureen and I signed it. Should we have had an expensive lawyer of our own check it out first? Probably. But it came in official and FedExed, with yellow tabs marked for us to put our names, and an envelope to send it back, no expenses. I mean, that's a professional operation! Mr. Berger is internationally known. Arlene and Bill told us to make sure Addison was repped. They told us without a gallery she might as well sell her art on a card table outside the Met. They told us it was only fair for the gallery to take 35 percent. Hell, some galleries even took 50 percent. They said it was boilerplate. We signed it. We just wanted Addison to be happy and protected. Was that so wrong?

What they didn't tell me until after she died is that Berger owns a percentage of everything Addison ever made. Like if my daughter drew some paper dolls in fourth grade? Berger controls those dolls. He calls all the shots on her estate. He can sell the paper dolls and take his cut, or he can cut 'em out and play with them. It's his call. Her art is his art. All her journals, her sketches, art that she didn't even sign . . . I guess that adds up. But I can't lie—what's left over is still one helluva lot of money! A fortune! I never thought my own kid was gonna take care of all my financial troubles. These checks come in every coupla months, and I just stare at the zeroes.

Maureen and I've used the money carefully. You're not gonna make us look bad about that, because you can't. I bought my houseboat. We paid Charlie's college tuition in one lump. We bought everybody's freedom to go their own way. But even when my girl was alive, she wanted to provide for us. I owed money. A little bit here and a little bit there. No big deal, but it had added up. Addison visited us at the end of that first summer, and she settled Maureen's and my credit cards, and she evened our debts. Snap of the fingers. Like magic.

ARLENE FIELDBENDER: When Addison came back to Rhode Island in August, Bill and I dropped by Bramble Circle to check in on her, to make sure that she was readjusting all right. It was evident things were not good. Addison looked worn out. She was sleeping a lot, she said, but not working much, unless she was at Lucy's house. She said she never could work calmly at home because it was a bad atmosphere.

"And they think I'm staying, Arlene," she whispered to me in the kitchen. "They think I'm going to finish high school here. But if I go back to South Kingstown after the summer I've had in New York, I'll die."

We assured Addison there'd been a miscommunication. But as it turned out, Maureen and Roy Stone had been in touch with Evelyn Tuttnauer. They were all concerned that Addison was drinking, which had counter-effects when taken with her Z. They wanted her home, to stabilize, however long that took.

MAUREEN STONE: Oh, it was all such a mess. We were very confused! Addison came back to us from New York so drained. All that I'd wanted was for her to get the city and its excesses out of her system. I thought that after the summer, she'd be happy to come home and jump back into the swing of South Kingstown High School. Senior year is special! You're so much older! The others look up to you! And Addison was a shoo-in to head *SKPades*, the school arts magazine, and to be on the homecoming committee. She was so stylish, you know. Addison was ambitious and talented, goodness, yes, and she'd had her fair share of troubles. But heavens, I still wanted her to be a girl, enjoying her life. Youth and innocence pass too quickly. "The big city will still be there!" I kept saying.

Jonah Lenox had graduated, of course. He was gone, living out in Colorado, and Addison missed him. He'd made her junior year safe and happy. But Lucy was here. And there were other nice, handsome boys to date.

Addison, however, was nothing but temper tantrums and attitude.

"What's there to do here? *What am I supposed to do here?*"

"What do you mean, what are you supposed to do here?" I'd say. "Just what you've always done, of course."

She was almost always at Lucy's, but she had an appointment with Dr. Tuttnauer every day. Just to complain, probably. She'd come back from her sessions and seem particularly furious with me, as if I'd trapped her. As if I'd singlehandedly created this jailhouse of a home and a torture of my normal hopes for her. So yes, we fought a bit that August. I'd say the sky was blue, and she'd tell me she didn't see any sky at all.

At some point, Addison got hold of a switchblade from Roy's toolbox, and she took to carving shapes into wood. The floor, the wall, the kitchen table. She just about ruined the house and scared us all to death besides! I'd wake up at three in the morning to find her carving *The Artist Is Starving* into the windowsill.

I was scared it would turn into an awful encore performance of what happened in Dartmouth. I was listening—eavesdropping, I guess you'd say—on Addison whenever she was talking to Lucy or Charlie or on the phone with her boyfriend, and I never heard Ida mentioned. But I could *sense* Ida. I could sense Addison thinking about her. Addison stopped getting dressed, for one. If she was at the house, she just slouched around in the same sweatpants and T-shirt, looking and smelling like a wreck. She was building some sort of gate on the lawn, she worked on it for four days solid, and then she abandoned it. Heavens, it looked as if Noah's ark had crashed there! Once when I was at work, she painted the entire living room—even the floor—in a purple so deep, it looked black. Another night she spray-painted the grass. Terrible, like a cartoon! She was rattling the bars of her cage, and she wanted everyone to know. Oh, but it was mortifying.

KARL TAEKO: One morning, I wake up and look through the window across the street. I turned to Ele and asked, "Are my eyes going, or did the Easter Bunny vomit all over Roy Stone's front lawn?"

"Neither," she said. "Addison's home."

CHARLIE STONE: Addison was being a brat, no doubt. Though that Crayola grass looked tight, actually. Everyone drove by to see it. Then all the grass died, and it looked like shit.

My sister didn't care. Her art or pranks, whatever you want to call them, were only for that moment. The one good part was that we were hanging out more. We'd sneak out at night—Mom and Dad had no idea. Addison was already kinda fan-page famous—getting her picture taken. Once we went to this club, Ultra, in Providence, and there were paparazzi, actual paps, tracking down a rumor that Addison and Zach had broken up, and she'd crawled home to lick her wounds.

Strange men with cameras were calling her name and following us down the street. Damn, that was a new one for me.

Addison and Charlie, out on the town, Providence, Rhode Island.
Ken Gilmore for *Time Out Providence*.

MAUREEN STONE: If she wasn't out at Lucy's or asleep, Addison would be in a near-comatose state, sleeping or whispering on the phone with Zach. One afternoon, I suggested taking her back-to-school shopping. It was a lovely summer day, perfect for strolling through the mall for some shopping, and I thought everything was fine, and then suddenly she snapped and said she wanted to go home.

"But we haven't even found your new school shoes," I said.

"Mom, you're killing me!" she yelled. In the middle of the food court, with everyone watching. "Do you really think I can handle trying on *loafers*? Do you truly think I care about *book bags*? Do you have a *clue* what my life has become?"

I felt terrible. But why did she have to make it all so complicated? Why couldn't she have just settled in and enjoyed her senior year? Was that really so much for any of us to ask?

ZACH FRATEPIETRO: I had flown over with some family and friends to stay for three weeks at Villa Divina, our place in Capri, while Addison was trapped in Rhode Island, spinning in circles. Once she called me, crying.

"Peace Dale sucks, my dad's a drunk, and my mom's a zombie, and they think I'm staying here for the school year. I'm jumping out the window this minute, Zach. You can't stop me."

I hoped that she was doing better than she sounded. Addison liked to be threatening; it was kind of like her little nudge to remind you she'd done it before. "Baby, you need to jump on a plane, not out the window. Come be with me," I told her. "You know I'd take such good care of you."

"No, I can't, I can't. Lucy's here, and my brother's here, and this is also my time with them."

"Then bring Lucy! She can date Alexandre! Bring Charlie. He's almost legal; he can chaperone us."

She laughed. We had a lot of conversations like that over those next weeks, but that's always as far as it got.

It was a catastrophe. Why would Addison's parents ever think she'd plant down in Rhode Island again? Sorry, but any delusion that Addison was dealing herself in for another year of that pokey 'burbs life after what she'd been doing in New York—it was pathetic. Addison was blowing up. Come September, she'd be spotlighted in every arts magazine that had a real circulation. Her life was about to become huge, and her parents didn't get the memo.

LUCY LIM: There's confusion on this point, right? Some people—cough-cough, Addy's parents—thought she'd do her senior year at South Kingstown. Other people—cough-cough, Arlene and Bill Fieldbender—thought she was just visiting her folks before moving back to the city for good, and throwing away the keys to Peace Dale.

I think the reason it's all a jumble is because Addy herself didn't know exactly what she wanted. She was delicate, health-wise. New York meant a lot of late nights, a lot of parties, and a general vibe of extreme living. Personally, I think Addison crept back to Peace Dale to get some very needed TLC, with sleep and rest, even while she was acting like Peace Dale was the worst place ever. She could have hopped an Amtrak or a Greyhound any time. But she didn't. She stayed for most of August, and a lot of those hours were spent in relative peace at my house.

"New York eats me up, it loves me so." That's a thing me and Addy used to say a lot. It's from *Where the Wild Things Are*. The monsters like to say it to Max. "I'll eat you up, I love you so!" We used that phrase for anything. Jewelry or frozen yogurt or boys, and I knew just what she meant.

In the end, the city did eat her up. Zach, Carine, Gil, Max Berger—they were all Addy-vores, each in a different way. On some level, maybe Addy understood that risk. Lame as Peace Dale might be, with our tract homes and fast food and playgrounds, it's a normal hometown. As broken as Roy and Maureen are, they loved her. At age eighteen, Addison couldn't really see her own cracks and fault lines, her fatal flaws, the weaknesses that would do her in. But she knew that the boring of Peace Dale sealed a lot of vice away from her. And she also knew that New York City opened it right up like a vein.

BILL FIELDBENDER: The truth? I saw an artist locking herself in the same prison cell that had almost killed her. Boring is also dangerous. Idle hands, et cetera. Addison had to get out of Peace Dale.

Once again, we got that ball rolling. Stepping in once again in mom and dad roles, when the real parents could not function. Arlene called in a favor and arranged for Addison to take some fall semester courses at Pratt. We also secured her a spot at Professional Children's School, so that she could finish her core curriculum and graduate from an accredited high school—while also working at her craft in a good facility with talented professors.

The truth is, Maureen and Roy Stone were ridiculously inept. Honestly, Addison would have done better being parented by a pair of sea cucumbers—and you can put that on record. Arlene and I don't have children of our own, and we saw Addison in some ways as a gift. The child we were meant to have. So it pained us, seeing how often Maureen and Roy took that extraordinary blessing for granted.

84 Court Street, Brooklyn, courtesy of Erickson McAvena.

VI.
ORDERLY GHOSTS

ERICKSON MCAVENA: I stayed way the hell away from my old Kentucky home that summer. I was in New York City almost the whole time, with some little hop-overs to Atlantic City, one trip up to Saratoga, one to The Pines on Fire Island, and that was it.

"You deal with getting yourself back to NYC, honey," I told Addison, "and I'll scope out our new sweet apartment." There was no way I'd live in a dorm again. Addison needed a roommate, and Teddy was a resident advisor that year, so he had a free room at Pratt. A single. I was the one who needed to go.

By the end of July, I'd wrangled us a two-bedroom above an Italian restaurant called Queen in Cobble Hill. It was a great location, between Livingston and Schemmerhorn. Fifth floor walk-up. Okay, it wasn't the Ritz, but on the top floor, there were skylights, a gas fireplace, plus the kitchen had a new oven and fridge, and we were close to the Borough Hall subway. Doable.

By Labor Day weekend, Addison was on the train back to me. We got Max Berger to co-sign our lease that Tuesday, and later that same afternoon, we were washing the walls and ripping up carpet. We loooved our new place. You could stand on the fire escape and smell the fresh-baked bread and pasta sauces wafting up from Queen's kitchen. Queen was expensive. Way out of our budget. We'd feast on the smells as we ate French fries from the McDonald's next door.

"We live on Court Street! We live high above the Queen!" Addison liked to proclaim. "But we are her most neglected subjects!" That's how we ended up calling our place The Queen's Shame.

But it was our palace. We gave it some dazzle. Once we'd repainted—every room a different shade of Addison's favorite purples, from glossy, deep midnight violet to soft blooming hydrangea to English lavender, we spruced it up with treasures from thrift shops and antique shops. We hit Brooklyn Flea and all the church sales. The jewel in our crown was the day we bought a shabby green velvet Victorian nine-foot-long sofa that we'd found at Housing Works.

Then Addison says, "We need to throw a housewarming!" And so we did. The epic housewarming. We called it "Hermaphor Night." You had to come as both your male and female self. Genius, right?

Addison and I wore black leggings and black T-shirts, and we tied ourselves together at the waist with kitchen twine.

"Synchronicity empowers," she'd say. We didn't look much alike—but we were about the same height, both a hair over five nine, and our names—Addison and Erickson. Inside, we were the shit-kicking duality. Our party crushed it, and then it was too much. I'd guess five hundred people in all, through the night? Sometimes it was packed like a transit car pulling into Grand Central.

STEPHANIE NORTON: I was hanging out with my big brother that weekend. I'd just come back from a college tour, and I was heading up to Choate afterward. Alexandre invited me to come with him to a party Zach's girlfriend was throwing. Addison and I are—were—the same age, and I guess I think of myself as fairly knowledgeable of New York. Been there, done that, got the swag. My family is connected, I grew up connected, I've done so many clubs and shows and parties and galas and benefits, it's how I mark my timelines—did I get my braces off before the Robin Hood benefit or after Young Friends of the Frick?

And even still, I'd never seen anything like Addison Stone, and I've never been to anything like that party she threw. She was this slim, dark shadow, as perfect as an object of art, but she was also full of life—demanding, hilarious, wild, elegant. I couldn't take my eyes off her. From a distance it seemed like she was standing perfectly still, but as you drew closer to her, you realized her life. She was listening, talking, thinking, her ideas were burning like meteors through her head.

I was too shy to speak to her. She singled me out. To this day I'm not sure why. "You must be Alexandre's sister."

"How do you know?"

"You have his same haughty melancholy in your eyes."

Haughty melancholy! I'd never heard myself described like that. Then she picked up a pen and her notebook, and she drew me, *sssswp ssswp ssswp,* in a quick sketch.

"That's so pretty!" I said. I was also shocked. It looked just like me. She *got* me. And she had done it with so little effort.

"I'da found you," she answered. I didn't know what she meant. Why would she have found me?

Later, she grabbed my number from Alexandre and texted me to come sit for her. Alexandre said I'd be a fool not to. If Addison Stone wanted to paint my portrait, I'd better drop everything and go to her. So I came down the next weekend and sat for the portrait that became *Being Stephanie*. She was so sweet—she took me out to dinner, she told me the story about her scars, and "Ida"—which was creepy, but the way Addison talked about it, somehow, it seemed normal-ish.

ERICKSON MCAVENA: The end of that night is a daze. At some point, a few of us were playing Twister—which kind of became the signature game of future parties. And then at a darker, later hour, our party went to hell in a hand-basket. Kids getting nekkid, kids pissing in our potted fern because the line to the one bathroom was too long. We had some drugs around, sure. Nothing serious. I myself was higher than a Georgia pine, but it was nothing I couldn't handle. Addison didn't drink or do drugs, since she was on such a serious scrip, plus her brain at rest was trippier than anywhere you get to on other substances. It was never as wild as they made it out to be. If that girl Danielle hadn't gotten hurt, nobody would ever have thought about that party again.

I'd never met Danielle Stanley. The girl who fell from the fire escape. I didn't even recall her face. But within minutes, TMZ was on it. They covered the story, adding in all kinds of scoops about Addison and Zach and their wicked partying ways.

Danielle Stanley was here in the city to study architecture. From what I heard, she'll never walk without a cane. A month after we visited her in the hospital, she moved back to Wisconsin. Addison was really upset about the whole thing. You know, I never even saw an ambulance? That whole night was way too notorious. And it sure didn't help Addison's reputation as a wild child.

Late-night Twister party at Court Street apartment, courtesy of Erickson McAvena.

ADDISON STONE (from her own recorded notes): I am now a New Yorker! Living the dream. I even bought myself one of those lame I ♥ NEW YORK T-shirts. Why not, right? I've seen the logo my whole life, and now here I am. Heart-ing it. It's kind of cosmic. But what a stupid mess of a weekend. Poor Danielle. If we hadn't had the party, she wouldn't have almost died, right? Erickson and I did a Good Samaritan drop-in with candy and flowers, and that actually felt worse, because Danielle was still feeling bad that she'd party-crashed. And then she really crashed! Anyway, I keep telling myself it's not my fault. But it's cruising on the edge of my fault. It's close enough to the edge of my fault that now I'll talk about other things.

What else, what else? Berger secured me studio space in Chelsea. I'm set up with my bank account and Visa card. No more mooching off Bank of Zach. Yes to that. Zach's open wallet did not exactly give me a crusading feminist feeling. Funny thing, my whole life all I ever did was worry about money, or listen to my folks fight about money, or feel humiliated at all the shabby parts of my life. So now my central life's worry has been wiped out. What do I worry about, if I can't worry about money? That is the burning question!

Here's my worry answer: the future. My future. My legacy. Crazy, since I've barely started. But I think about it. I want people to say, "That's the grandmother of—" whatever I end up becoming. I want to walk through my retrospective at the MoMA at age eighty-three in a long scarlet dress and fire-engine-red lipstick and have everyone whisper, "Addison Stone really means something. To herself, and in the world."

So okay. Big plans! To be continued!

ERICKSON MCAVENA: Addison's work studio was at Seventh Avenue and 18th Street. Top floor of the Hellmuth Building. She loved the studio because a Dutch artist she admired, Karel Appel, had once lived in the same building. Her address was also one building away from the studio where Willem de Kooning had painted all his life.

"Ghosts of Dutchmen are all around," Addison would say. "Orderly ghosts. I've known disorderly ghosts, Erickson, and believe me, my Dutch ghosts are better." I never knew if she was joking with me on that.

She was painting Stephanie Norton, and she was also working on a few studies for a painting she'd do some months later, of her therapist, Roland Jones. She liked offbeat faces—she enjoyed learning more about a person through the rendering of their face.

Addison thought Roland—"Doc," she called him—was a smart therapist because he was a really careful listener. I told her whatever, she just wanted to paint his Old Wise Man beard. That girl could log in some hard hours painting. I don't think I ever met anyone who worked harder. I'd have to text her reminders to come home. Then she'd drag herself back bone-tired to the apartment. I'd have soup, mac & cheese, all her comfort food ready. But she liked to work.

Zach Frat was the unwanted distraction. He was always putting pepper in the gumbo, trying to bribe Addison into going out with him to the clubs—and you can't fool me; I knew half the reason was to get his face in the paper with his It Girl arm candy.

He'd show up all hours at the Court Street apartment, looking for her. He could be such a pain in the ass. "Why is Addison still at the studio?" he'd ask me. "Text her, tell her we want her to come home." Like I was the butler.

Or, he'd give me the sad version: "Do you think she's forgotten about me?"

Or, the paranoid version: "Do you think there's another guy?"

Or, the bro-to-bro version: "Erickson, give it to me straight. Do you know what's up with Addison? Does she ever talk shit about me? 'Cause if you know, you gotta tell me!"

I never knew what Addison saw in Zach. There's a Southern saying—you can't know the depth of the well by the handle of the pump. Zach was a shiny handle. But there was no depth to that guy.

Addison and Erickson in the kitchen of their apartment, courtesy of Marie-Claire Broyard.

ZACH FRATEPIETRO: Look, I understand artists, okay? I was raised by them, no kidding; all my babysitters either smelled like sculpting clay or turpentine. I get their narcissism and their insecurity. But I'd done everything for Addison. I'd set her up huge. I watched that Addison ate real breakfasts and took her Zyprexa. I made sure she was checking in with her therapist, Tuttnauer—"Nut Tower," Addison called her. And also with her New York therapist.

"Shake, rattle, and Roland Jones," I'd remind her whenever she had an appointment. I'd even stay in the waiting room. Just so she had me to lean on after. She was ashamed of her therapy. She hated being reminded that she needed it. But I never minded. Artists and shrinks go together like milk and cookies.

And I made sure that Addison wasn't in her studio till four in the morning. I'd break those nine-, ten-hour work sessions just as much as Erickson did. And I did it by getting her out to meet friends. When I look back, I realize I'd put my own life on hold. I was a glorified gardener, pruning and watering and watching for every new mood blossom on the Addison Stone tree.

All I wanted was some respect. All I wanted was for her not to jerk me around with prima donna behavior. But power corrupts, right?

Like maybe I'd get on her case—just a little bit—for not showing up to somewhere. So I'd call her and say something like, "Hey, where are you, Addison? We are all at Blue Ribbon; it is so-and-so's birthday party. Thought you were coming to this."

And she'd go, "Oh, yeah, I'll be there in twenty. I'm leaving right now."

Then an hour later, I'd call her. "Where are you? You said you were just leaving?"

"Oh, yeah, sorry, Zach. I'm not coming anymore."

And I'd be like, "Fucking hell, Addison! We haven't even ordered dinner because we're all sitting around with our thumbs up our asses, waiting for you!"

Soon it got to be a habit. If she felt too cornered, then it was: "Fuck you, Zach, I didn't come to New York City to be your trophy! I came here for my own trophies! If I fail, then what's left for me? I'll be an assistant at some second-rate gallery in Providence or Boston. Unlike you, I can't rely on my million-dollar trust fund."

Addison saw her life as all or nothing. Winner take all, loser eats dust. I tried not to step in the ring with her, but it was hard. I'm part Italian, so it's natural for me to get my dukes up. We'd fight, and we'd say nasty things to each other. Addison liked to throw dishes. I liked to punch walls. But I also like to make up. And I was always looking for the compromise. Not Addison. She'd never go to Blue Ribbon once she decided she didn't want to go. She believed in doing only what she felt like doing.

Eventually I knew that her selfish side wasn't good for me, and I had to let her go. So I did.

MARIE-CLAIRE BROYARD: However Zach needs to make it right in his head about how he and Addison ended, let me tell you, it didn't end like that. Their breakup *crushed* him. Here's the short version of what happened. When Addison got back to New York City that fall, Zach's rich-boy glamour didn't hold the same appeal. So, *thud.* She dropped him. And she didn't exactly tell him, either. Not straight. Not clean. Not the way she should have.

I'd been out with Zach plenty of times that September through October, when Addison was supposed to show, and she'd just stand him up. And he'd lose his mind. "Where is she, goddammit? She always does this!"

I have to admit, this was the first time I'd seen Zach unravel over a girl. Here's Zach Frat, modelizer, a hundred different girls in love with him, and Addison Stone had the arrogance to *dump* his ass. But dump his ass she did. Actually, it was more like a series of a hundred little dumps. Maybe she'd find something at Film Forum she just *had* to get to, or there was a flash sale, or a Phoenix concert.

She'd call me and say, "Let's go see the Renee Dijkstra retrospective at The New Museum, and then hit Jemma on the Bowery for biscuits and gravy—and pleeeease don't tell Zach. He's expecting me to be at the Gansevoort."

Now I love Zach to *pieces*, but he's not the fastest boat in the harbor. He hadn't realized that his scene had lost its luster. Addison's boredom was obvious to everybody but Zach, whose brain would never, ever sail into the realization that she'd had enough of flitting around and wasting time being fabulous at the best parties. But when Addison was done, darling, she was *done*.

Being Stephanie by Addison Stone, courtesy of the Bellamy Collection.

CARINE FRATEPIETRO: I will speak a little bit about this, but I must remind you that on this topic, our lawyers have advised me to be brief. With regard to Addison's relationship with my son, I was always quite protective of Addison. "Please do not attend Addison Stone's next opening," I told him. She had finished *Being Stephanie* along with some other pieces, and we were showing them, with a very few other select artists, at Berger Gallery. It was a carefully curated show, and I didn't want it turned into a media circus with Zach's presence. Addison's mental stability was also something to consider.

"But I discovered Addison," he said to me. "It's my opening, too."

"Nobody discovered her," I said. "Do not distress each other. Let it end gracefully."

Yes, I was interfering. I was asking him to step away from her. The fight for Addison became a refrain with us. Zach was still in love with Addison, who'd cruelly and unceremoniously called it off with him. As a mother, I ached to protect my son. But Addison, as a young artist, was a votive. The flame of a votive is small and relatively unguarded, and it also must be protected. In the turmoil of Zach's own emotions, he himself could not be called on to respect that flame. And so I asked him not to go near it.

Do I blame Zach for subsequent mistakes with regard to Addison Stone? I do. That situation was being mishandled months before the tragedy. But again, my family has been advised not to speak in depth about this, so please excuse me if I don't.

ERICKSON MCAVENA: Teddy and I cooked up a theory that Addison and Zach fell in hate with each other. And their hate affair was a lot harder on 'em than love. Our theory went like this: Zach had everything that Addison needed—education and money and connections. But Addison had the only thing Zach's renowned mommy really valued—genius. So if the brilliant Addison loved Zach, then it was proof to Carine that he was worthy. When she broke it off, it reinforced all of his insecurity about himself as a false, flashy wanna-be in the art world.

The break-up was a mess. Addison's leading trait is fearlessness. Zach's is bravado. Addison could be ruthless, too. She had to win. And so did Zach. When they turned against each other, boy, did the fur fly.

There's this one night when me and Teddy and Addison were hanging in the apartment, lazing around, watching a movie, and all of a sudden Addison says, "I know! I know how to get him!" She'd been brewing on it. She got Teddy inspired to help her. Next thing I know, the two of them were building a fake gossip website.

It looked so real! Except every headline was about Zach: "Style Tips from Dirtbag New Yorkers." Or "Art Scion's Playboy Son Confesses: How I Lose My Family's Fortune at 2M a Year." With private pictures of Zach from Addison's own stash.

Teddy's a part-time web programmer, and he put up the site live.

Zach got his lawyer to remove it, but not before there'd been over a hundred thousand hits. I think Zach took Addison's punch straight to the gut. Actually, I know so—I was with Addison when he called her, late that same night. Zach can string the curse words together from here to Sunday. On and on he went. But underneath it, he was hurting. I was surprised, too. I know it was one of those "heat of the moment" ideas, but it was a mean, childish thing of her and Teddy to do. I should have interfered. Somebody needed to be the grown-up.

Addison never lost a chance to call Zach a spoiled trust puppy. She always wanted him to "see himself for who he is." It was like she needed to force-feed Zach cruelty truth serum. I knew there'd be more twists on the Zach-and-Addison revenge show. I just never could have predicted how destructive it'd all get. Could anyone?

FROM THE FIRST MOMENT that I embarked on this biography, I'd figured that my biggest hurdle would be to secure the cooperation of Lincoln Reed. So as I started gathering interviews— living for a couple of weeks in Peace Dale, Rhode Island, then traveling to Hong Kong so that I could sit down eye to eye with Max Berger, or catching up with Zach Frat on the EuroRail before the Art Paris Art Fair—I knew that my project was a soufflé that would collapse if I couldn't pin down Lincoln.

After Addison died, there was a rumor Lincoln had left the country to live in Nepal. Since Lincoln and Zach both were "people of interest" in the investigation, I figured I'd need to chase the mystery—to Nepal, or to anywhere. Neither Lincoln nor Zach had an alibi. Both could be placed in New York City on the night that she died.

People speculated that Lincoln had gone into deep hiding until he could get his name cleared. It made sense—Zach had the advantage of money, and the moment there was a breath of suspicion about his part in Addison's death, he lawyered up. Lincoln didn't have that fortune cushion. So he had to vanish.

Finally, late that spring, I got a break. I was tipped off that

Lincoln Reed had been summoned to New York City's Precinct 13 for questioning about his whereabouts on July 28th. But by the time I showed, he was gone. I checked in with Lincoln's friends, his regular hangouts, his sublet on Elizabeth Street. He was a phantom. Without Lincoln, there was no book.

That same night, I got an email from the account of "I. DaBristol." The name was both an alias and a reference to Ida. Whoever was sending this mail, this person knew Addison well. The note was only a Sag Harbor address and a time to meet—a 7 A.M. breakfast at the American Hotel.

I woke up before sunrise the next morning, drove the two hours to Sag Harbor, walked into the hotel, and there he was, almost unrecognizable: thick beard, shaggy hair, and skin tanned three shades darker than any photo I'd ever seen of him.

When we sat down for breakfast, Lincoln ordered for us both and also paid the check—he'd said this was "his town." Throughout the meal, he seemed at ease, speaking candidly about Sophie Kiminski, whom he'd learned had just gone back into rehab. "Sophie's the King Midas of tragedy," he said. "Every life she touches is the worse for it."

It also came clear that Lincoln was cooperating with authorities, and he swore he had nothing to hide "from a legal standpoint. But there are also things I want to tell you. And if you're painting a portrait of Addison Stone, I'd better melt into it, right? Or else it won't look like her in the end."

VII.
"THERE'S ALWAYS SO MUCH TRAFFIC AROUND HIM."

Lincoln Reed at his studio on Elizabeth Street, courtesy of the estate of Addison Stone.

LINCOLN REED: I met Addison Stone on a photo shoot for *Catch* magazine. By then, both of us had a few of these arty-interview puff pieces under our belts. You make fun of that stuff until you get invited to do it. It's selling out, but it gets you meetings, it gets people wanting to know more about you. They crave the unimportant details—if you eat Cheerios for breakfast, if you have a cat, parrot, or goldfish, if you drink coffee or smoke or listen to music while you paint. But opening yourself up keeps you relevant, and it keeps your public fascinated. That's important.

I'd just finished a semester at Arti di Firenze in Florence. I'd done a show that traveled from Florence to Venice to Rome, and then it continued to London and New York. I called it my "poisons" phase. I'd been obsessed with themes of noxious gases, chemical warfare—how poisons inhabit and destroy the body. It's the topography of the human body in wartime. Not exactly a feel-good theme. So I wasn't sure if I wanted to sell myself out to *Catch* as a pretty boy. To tell you the truth, I was feeling ambivalent about the whole thing.

Addison was late to the shoot. I could feel myself getting pissed off. Why should I be kept waiting for this month's egomaniacal It Girl? Then the freight elevator opened, and there she was, with her saucer eyes and legs like a colt. She strides into the space, pulling out her elastic, and this mane of black hair falls—*swoosh*—down her back.

"I didn't know I'd be sharing the spotlight with you," she told me later. But I knew she was annoyed that I was annoyed. Ads didn't have much poker face. She took her sweet time in hair and makeup. So I gave it right back to her. I ordered a pizza for delivery, I texted with some friends. Then Addison began changing her T-shirts in front of me, making sure I was looking at her. Ha, and I was. We were both being obnoxious, just to see how the other one would respond. Kid games. The photographer, Zoe, wanted to kill us. She didn't get the shot, either. Not then, anyway.

ZOE SKLOOT: I was the principal photographer on the *Catch* shoot when Addison Stone met Lincoln Reed. They were the newest talent in New York City, and, footnote, they were both gorgeous. A photographer's dream. I could also tell in a heartbeat they'd fallen hard for each other. Not that they were going to let us see that. They were both piss and vinegar that day. But love was in the air. Addison couldn't keep her eyes off Lincoln, and every time she spoke, I watched his neck flush red as a cranberry.

The chemistry between them was incredible; the sparks were almost visible. Addison kept her cool but wouldn't stay still. She kept slithering into different outfits and changing the music and dancing—Bossa Nova, French Nouvelle, Arcade Fire, Daft Punk. Cranking it up, claiming every inch of space in my studio.

And the more Addison swanned, "I like this, I love that," or "I don't think that's working," the more Lincoln stayed perfectly quiet and hard-eyed.

That final image! I'd taken some cute shots but I hadn't gotten what I wanted, and I was frustrated, sort of defeated. Their connection, that chemistry—it was just outside my reach. And then we were packed up and done, in the freight elevator, and all I had was my little Olympus Stylus slung on my shoulder—and suddenly, Addison stepped back, so that she was standing very close in front of Lincoln. She was looking up and away, on a clean angle as he stared straight ahead. There's the million-dollar moment. Yet you can see beyond a shadow of a doubt that each one consumes the other.

Interesting thing about that shot, which was the one we ended up using for *Catch*, are that Lincoln's eyes are hidden by sunglasses, and Addison's eyes by the way she's turned. But you can read their intimacy. It's like they know they're almost together, and destined for each other.

Lincoln and Addison.
Zoe Skloot for *Catch* magazine.

From: **Addison Stone** <addisonstoneart@gmail.com>
Date: Oct 16 at 11:38 PM
Subject: random rage etc.
To: Lucy Lim <lucygracelim@gmail.com>

Hey, LL—

finish your paper on poor ole marginalized Margaret Fuller, you giant
nerd?
Well, enough about you, ha ha!
Newsy piece: this afternoon on a photo shoot for an art mag,
I met this guy Lincoln Reed.
He's a "name" in the art world even if it means nothing to you.
All I can say: MAJOR PRICK ALERT.

You know how when I first met The Lenox, after he finally stopped by
the art room,
I was like, oh yeah. This is happiness. This is happening.

Then, with Zach Frat—how I'd seen him at the Berger opening last
summer?
And I instantaneously felt the sizzle that we'd be together?

So take that excellent karma & find the opposite of it.
That is Lincoln Reed.

Example. You remember that time
when we went out to dinner at Basta Pasta in Little Compton and we
ordered the Mexican calamari and we got the shocking surprise of food
poisoning?

Lincoln Reed is Mexican calamari.

As in, he looks pretty hot with salsa.
But he is actually vomit-worthy.

Seriously, I would rather vomit calamari down my chest all night long
than SPEND ONE MINUTE WITH THIS ARROGANT GUY!!!

Ok now I feel better. His art is cool.
I give him that.
He's doing all this crazy shit about poison through the centuries.
Deadly plants through mustard gas.
I'm kind of hugely professionally jealous.

Enough about this guy! Why am I still telling you about him?

You still coming to visit me for Halloween?
I miss you tons, Lu!
x!o!

LINCOLN REED: Addison and I met up again the next weekend
at the Klempf Art pre-party. October 21st. It was cold and crisp
and a deep blue night. I knew she was on the list. I was by the
door as she came in. We'd been strangers, feral animals circling
each other at the photo shoot. But we had something. There'd
been too much kick, too much sparring to be nothing.

So I got bold. Walked right up to her and looked her
square in the eye and said, "Hey, Addison. Good to see you
again. I'm heading to the bar, if you want a drink?"

And she put that raven-black stare right back on me and
said, "Red wine, please. But only if you're drinking with me."

I came back with two glasses of red. She looked incredible. She was never a girl who wore heels or frilly dresses.
Her dress was plain black, risqué short, with a band of bright
purple on the bottom. She'd sewed on the band herself. She
said that this particular shade was "her" color. She smelled
great, too. Like the beach. A pure scent.

I don't know why I also got myself a glass of red. To show

her we had something in common? Even though I never
drink red. I don't drink at all, actually. And neither did she.
We had a good laugh about that later.

From: **Addison Stone** <addisonstoneart@gmail.com>
Date: Oct 22 at 2:11 AM
Subject: ok scratch that
To: Lucy Lim <lucygracelim@gmail.com>

my g-chat is messed up today.
But here's my update on Lincoln Reed.
Ooookay, I went back and looked at that note I sent you last week.

And now . . . drumroll . . .
Presenting my new thoughts on Lincoln Reed.

(with apologies for being so flat-out clueless.)

Analogy correction:
Meeting Lincoln was like being thrown into a waterfall.
Not into calamari food poisoning hell.

Because . . . he's SPECTACULAR.

Lulu, you need to meet him. You need to be around him.
You need to look at him.
You need to hear his voice.
He's got this slow, sleepy way of talking.
You'd start to take off your clothes like a sex zombie just to be near it.

Everyone wants to be near Lincoln.
Everyone presses around to hear what he's got to say.
They want to know what he knows. There's always so much traffic
around him.
And his art! Harsh, brutal, violent, real, in-your-face.

His dad was Robard Reed, a sculptor (I'd never heard of him either, but apparently, a big deal).

His mom was one of many girlfriends—the last girlfriend, because he killed himself at age sixty-one.

The same year Lincoln was born.

And he's got all these half sisters and brothers. So exotic! I felt lame and small town,

I wanted to pretend my dad was a spy or something . . .

Anyway. Lulu. I think I'm in it. Deep.

(Full disclosure he's sleeping next to me. Chastely. For now. Shhh.)

Got 1,000,000 things else to tell you, but I'm late for this stupid Pratt writing class. I've pretty much dropped all my non-art classes at Pratt. They're all doomed to be a total waste of time.

Miss you!

x!o!

LINCOLN REED: That night, we took off from Klempf together, and I didn't leave Addison's side for the next ten days. We walked all the way down the East Side, over the Manhattan Bridge. We kissed at the top of the bridge.

And right there, we knew.

It was that same week of the hurricane. Her apartment on Court Street was Zone 2. We were okay. Lying in bed, listening to rain in sheets, and the wind howling, we were like two refugees in our own private pocket of the world. By Halloween, the storm was done, and we rolled out of bed and got dressed and checked out the damage in Cobble Hill and Red Hook. Addison was dressed as Amy Winehouse, with the eyeliner and the beehive, and I said I was Jim Morrison—just a string of beads around my neck. Then Erickson joined up in a flannel shirt as Kurt Cobain. We were the Doom Trifecta. The city was waterlogged and wounded, but people were out in it, going about their business, surviving together. We walked around, talked art. It was great.

That night, I ordered a huge Italian feast from Queen, and we all pounced on it, ravenous. Over that next week, I made a point to get to know her crew. We spilled our histories. It was obviously important to Addison that I was approved by Teddy and Erickson. My understanding was that Zach Frat hadn't been much liked.

At the end of every night, right before she went to sleep, Addison always gave me the biggest smile and said, "If I leave before you, baby, don't you waste me in the ground."

I knew she was quoting something, but I didn't know what—turned out to be an Iron and Wine song, "Naked as We Come." Addison could quote a million plays and poems and song lyrics. She especially loved Amy Winehouse—her decadence and her fatalism. Addison never saw the tragedy. She could only see the beauty in a Winehouse song. Not the doom. I hear Amy Winehouse whenever I see Addison's *Chandelier Girl* clip. Sure, she could have died. Easy. But you never think about death when you see that clip. You only think about beauty.

LUCY LIM: Addy and I would always check in—by phone or text or email—every single day. Usually phone. I'd start the morning with a Starbucks coffee in my car in the student parking lot, right before homeroom bell. Just to find out how everything was going. She liked to do it, too. She needed those rituals.

So when I didn't get anything from Addy for three days, not even for Halloween, not pictures, nada, I was worried. Whenever I didn't hear from Addy, my mind jumped back to the last time she fell way out of touch, and next thing I heard she was in the loony bin. On day three, I called Bill and Arlene, and then we basically sent texts and called her cell until she finally texted back: stop! all good! lincoln!

Lincoln and Addison napping on the velvet couch, Court Street apartment, courtesy of Erickson McAvena.

MARIE-CLAIRE BROYARD: Someone had seen Addison and Lincoln kissing at the Klempf Art benefit. The gossip spread around New York like a kudzu vine. Zach had been holding out hope, you know. But not after he caught the rumor.

And one night soon after, Zach came storming over to my place, red-faced. Bellowing like a bull. I was living on 88th and Madison, in this la-dee-da co-op building, and I got three noise complaints, all because of Zach.

He was out of his mind. "I can't get hold of her, she's with Lincoln, she won't return my calls, it's like I never existed, she's such a bitch!" Pounding the wall, but I could see he was teary.

"She used me, MC. She promised—she swore all she needed was time. Time with *him*."

I was like, "Sweetie, let's go shopping first thing tomorrow. Let's snap up every color cashmere at Loro Piana." That's where Zach and I understand each other—in retail therapy.

But he couldn't get it together. He drank the rest of my scotch, and then he sort of collapsed in a stupor on my sofa. Finally after midnight, I was starving, so we wobbled over to The Restaurant at The Mark Hotel for poached artichokes. Zach is a pathetic drunk. Back at my apartment, I ran him a bath like a baby. He sat in my claw-foot tub, and I bathed him, and then we had sex—*charity sex*, I should mention. Sweet and comforting, but charity sex is never the solution, is it? Unfortunately, sometimes that's what you do when you're not sure what else to do. The next morning, I hate to admit it, but I sort of threw him out like a dog.

But I was walking a fine line, balancing my time with Zach and my time with Addison—she was coming uptown quite a bit, doing some studies for my portrait that would become her beautiful painting *MCB*. She was *so* giddy in love with Lincoln, she never even mentioned Zach. I was always so nervous that Zach would come around while Addison was over.

Even to this day, Addison still haunts Zach. And I don't want to talk myself into a corner here, but whatever happened that night she died, Zach was in town. And there are question marks *all over* that relationship, what with all that one-upmanship, and all the ongoing nonsense between them.

ADDISON STONE (from *ArtUnite*): In the fall, I fell in love. I was painting happy things. My brain was in dreamland— I wanted to feed grapes to my boyfriend. And so that's why I started some pencil studies that would become the painting of my friend Marie-Claire, who is so refined and delicate.

But I'd also met Dom and Cam Lutz, the brainpower behind some really avant-garde and very cool installations that had been cropping up all over the city. I'll always love street art and pranks and creating a spectacle. So we conjured up this idea to do a billboard collage of twelve people who'd been imprisoned for their political beliefs, all around a Thanksgiving dinner table. From Bobby Sands to Aung San Suu Kyi to Mahatma Gandhi to Maria Alekhina from Pussy Riot. We wanted to give thanks for these people. Look, I didn't want to make money from it. I didn't want to sell it privately. I didn't even want to sign it. I wanted to make public art. From me, for everyone. That's the beauty of it.

Dom and Cam were famous vandals. They were pulling fun, big-scale stunts. Their latest thing was screwing around with statues of old war heroes. You know those statues you see in the parks? They'd spray-paint 'em, dress them up so it looked like they were all in ballet costumes.

Once the Lutz boys got on board, we assembled the collage with blow-up photographs and decided to plaster up the whole installation at the Queens Midtown Tunnel, which links midtown Manhattan with Central Queens and the Long Island Expressway. It's a thick traffic artery. And Dom had found an empty billboard. If a corporation is running an ad on a billboard and you replace it with your own shit, you're screwed. The company has a big temper tantrum, and then their lawyers make you take it down. But an empty billboard? Gold mine. We determined that the least amount of traffic was between three and five in the morning. Good weather, no rain. Just cold November. All systems go.

There's a rush of getting an installation up before day-break, sweaty and hoping not to be caught. Then seeing it, truly seeing it, for the first time in public. It's sorcery! And knowing how pissed Max Berger was going to be—hell, yeah, that added to the fun. But we had a few hair-raising moments. I slipped out of my harness, for one. But all's well that ends with you alive to see your work, and not getting caught in the process.

MAUREEN STONE: Addison called me very early in the morning, the same morning that she'd put up that bill-board. She was hardly ever in touch anymore. And she'd been ignoring my emails and voice mails, all my questions about if she might be coming home for Thanksgiving. She *said* I nagged her. Lord knows, I didn't mean to nag. Of course I wanted to give her the space she needed. Gracious, I was too scared of her not to give it.

"I almost died on the freeway, Mom!" she said. Then she told me she'd slipped out of her harness and fallen. She hadn't been hit by a car, but she'd had to scramble off the highway, fast.

My heart was thudding in my chest. I had no idea what she was trying to tell me. Only later did she start from the beginning.

"I'm okay, I promise! Some bumps and bruises, that's all." She was laughing, out of breath. "I'm okay!"

I didn't know what it was all about, but I understood that she'd had a moment of pure fear. And I was so grateful that, inside that fear, she'd called me. And I was even more happy that *she* was glad to be alive, but now always when I think back over on it, I wonder if maybe she was just glad she'd lived long enough to put up her art.

LUCY LIM: I came down to New York to see Addy for my Thanksgiving break. She was on a high. She'd finished that painting of Marie-Claire, and she'd learned that it had been selected for display in the Armory exhibit. She was wild about Lincoln Reed. The *Thanksgiving* piece had gone up that previous week, and it was viral, and she was being whispered about, along with the Lutz brothers. The only thing Addison liked better than being gossiped about was being whispered about. She was happy, but not manic.

Justine and *Seventeen* and *Teen People* magazines were all knocking, too. Everyone wanted to know more about the pretty girl who painted *Being Stephanie* and *MCB*. Addy was catnip. It bothered her that she was also starting to be called "Girl Banksy." You know Banksy? That guy who pulls the public hoax stunts? I didn't. Addy had to show me his stuff—she didn't think they had much parallel. The Banksy shout-outs were still great press for her. But like all Addy highs, it ended with a crash. And in this case, I was there, and the name of that crash was Jonathan Coulsen.

MCB by Addison Stone, courtesy of the Broyard family.

AUTHOR'S NOTE

JONATHAN COULSEN, WHO DECLINED to be interviewed for this book, is an American-born art critic whose blog, Juggernaut, is known for its provocative pieces and scathing critiques of international art and culture. While Coulsen's sharply contentious opinions have sometimes been derided as "party trick prose," his criticism has always drawn attention for its nerve and poison-dart targeting. While Coulsen is not affiliated with any one philosophy of art, he is occasionally dismissed as an "old-school conservative." Rights to republish Coulsen's piece, "Bohemian Bauble: A Closer Look at Addison Stone," were denied.

LINCOLN REED: God bless Lucy Lim for being with us over Thanksgiving, the same weekend that we found out about Jonathan Coulsen's article. Erickson had left, gone to Teddy's house in Virginia. So it was just us three, Lucy, Ads, and me, making a kickass "Friendsgiving." That was what Lucy called it. Stuffed portobello mushrooms, maple-roasted Brussels sprouts, key lime pie. None of us were cooks, not like Erickson, and the kitchen was tiny, but nothing mattered except that we were all together.

At the time I was just in it, you know? Just stupidly assuming it would be the first of dozens of "Friendsgivings" like that one, until we were old and gray.

Late that afternoon, I'm on my phone, and I see Addison's name in my Twitter feed, with a link to Coulsen's blog. Jonathan Coulsen's a big, swinging dick of an art critic. One of the whales. Everyone knows when he's showing up at your opening, and everyone listens when he barks. And at the same time that I click the link, thinking it's going to be Coulsen sending out some love for Ads, I yell out—wishing too late that I hadn't—"Hey, listen to this!" Mistake.

She'd have found it anyway. But to this day I always kick myself for being the messenger.

LUCY LIM: A lot of people thought that Addy could have been the next Lucien Freud, easy. But this guy Coulsen was determined to smack her down just because she was young and hadn't been to some fancy art school and didn't know technique or tradition—basically, that she was just a kid.

At least he admitted Addy's portraits weren't just eye-catching because she was. But the gist of his whole rant was that she was image over substance, a bright and shiny poseur in the street art scene—that the *Thanksgiving* billboard stunt was just a pretty social climber's way of getting in with the Lutz brothers, who were somehow more "real." Oh, and he said she was too young to have perfected her technical skill, and she hadn't studied under anyone significant, and if she wanted to be a good little portrait painter, she should go get mentoring from the greats. On and on. Bitchy and cutthroat.

Addy always told me, "I never read up on what people are saying about me." But that was a lie. She read everything. She was curious about opinions—from Nobody in Crappytown's all the way up to Jonathan Coulsen's. His take-down knocked her hard that night. She didn't eat dinner. She opened some wine, which for her was always a horrible idea, while Lincoln and I pretended we'd forgotten about the whole thing, and tried to be all "la-la-la, what shitty review?"

LINCOLN REED: Addison Stone was a *kid*. New to New York. Talent like hers can make people seem older than their years, especially to someone like Coulsen. She wasn't ready for

Coulsen's attack. But I also knew Ads. In just over a month, I felt like I already had a sea-deep knowledge of this girl. I'd look at those long ridged scars on her wrists, and wonder about her. Wonder if she really was doing okay, if she was really doing better here in this moment. Wonder how much she was hiding from us all.

Anyway, that Friday morning after Thanksgiving, I had only one goal—to get Addison's mind off Coulsen. And I remembered how Ads and Lucy had occasionally talked about this guy Jonah, and how they used to go road-tripping with him. So I have this '79 Pontiac GTO. Vintage. Dove gray. I bought it when I turned eighteen. Driving my car is what I like to do instead of drink or drugs or therapy.

"Boys and cars," she said when I suggested it. Not even really there. I don't think she'd slept. Then she perked up. "If we went somewhere, where would we go?"

I didn't tell her. I just told her to get ready. Lucy came, too, and we drove the three-plus hours straight to Sag Harbor, where I grew up.

I took Addison and Lucy to my favorite places in Sag. At the American Hotel, where my dad used to hang out, we all ordered eggs Benedict breakfasts and pots of cocoa. I'd never seen Addison so insecure.

"Coulsen's right," she kept saying. "I'm not trained, I'm a punk. I won't have a career, I'm not building a legacy, I'm a trend, I'm confetti, I'm nothing."

I didn't know what to say. But Lucy leaned forward and squeezed Addison's hand, and she said, "Look, Addy, if you doubt this one guy, you will doubt everyone all the time. And I'm not even talking as your friend. I'm talking as a fan of your art. Do not let some cranky old man tell you what you are. I want to see more from you."

That was what did it for me, with Lucy. I felt like I had total clarity on how Addison had gotten through her childhood, with Lucy on her side. Watching her, knowing her, saying exactly the right thing when Ads needed to hear it most. Pretty powerful.

Lincoln and Addison eating breakfast, courtesy of Lucy Lim.

MAXWELL BERGER: Coulsen's piece stank up our investment in Addison. We had to act fast. I called in some favors. When one of my up-and-comers gets smacked with criticism that threatens to sink them, the trick is confidence. Bring the artist into the center. Sell harder. Then liking or disliking the art is only a matter of opinion. Not a verdict.

I dialed a connection to *Mirror Mirror* to spotlight Addison in their "One to Watch" section. It was a one-pager. The title copy read "GENUINE STONE." It was an introduction of

Addison in the mainstream press. With some copy about her high-wire public art, her billboards, her boyfriends.

My stroke of genius—I had just signed another artist, Etien Koort, who was also doing a lot of portraits. Koort's got a very styled, jet-set approach to young New York, and he'd been after Addison to do her portrait. Let me tell you, that article went down just right. With the painting, Addison looked like a class act again, like one of those old 1970s Hollywood-type stars. We "accidentally" leaked the Koort painting, exhibiting it months before it came out in February—and then I sold it to a Hollywood bad boy.

It did what we wanted and put the attention back on Addison as somebody we all wanted to see more of. But Addison herself? She was angry, and she came at me.

"You used me. You made me into an object. I'm not a part-time artist, part-time publicity stunt. You can't just decide when I should be controversy and when I need to be some kind of glamour kitten."

She started bad-mouthing me around town. Maybe she had a point. I didn't care. Bigger things were at stake.

Glamour Portrait of Addison Stone by Etien Koort, courtesy of T. Jay Gerhardt.

ERICKSON MCAVENA: I can draw a line in the sand from the Koort portrait to when Addison decided to rob Bergdorf Goodman's.

She was a fearless artist, but that was nothing compared with what a ballsy thief she was. The summer before, we both were so flat broke we'd pour Pabst Blue Ribbon on cornflakes for dinner. So damn poor we knew which hotel conventions were serving complimentary breakfasts. Once we hit up a Marriott to steal the tiny shampoos and mouthwashes from the cleaning ladies' carts. But by fall, Addison had sold her *Billfold* series, and she'd sold *Being Stephanie.* So I thought she wanted to make purchases.

She'd planned it all out before. I didn't know that. She scampered into the dressing room with an armload of outfits. Later she told me she'd packed this little pair of hedge clippers to remove the security tags. She stuffed the new clothes into her backpack and replaced them with something close enough that she'd found at the Salvation Army. On the surveillance cameras, you can't see what's going on. It looks like she's marching in and out with the same items. She wasn't. Total damage was almost ten thousand dollars.

"That's a felony, Addison," I told her.

"That's all right," she answered.

"You're crazy."

"Oh, I'm sending it back. I just wanted to show them how easy it is."

She was proud of herself. I remember thinking, *Sweet Jesus, who's gonna cut this girl a switch?* It was like Addison had no feeling that this was a bad thing or a wrong thing. Especially when she sent Bergdorf back four boxes marked, *Stolen and Returned, xo Addison.* She had to have her own little catawampus. She had to get that mischief out of her system.

STARGAZER LUZ: Well, right off I should say that's not my real name. I wish! Stargazer is how everyone around here knows me. First I was known as Robard Reed's daughter. Now I'm known as Lincoln Reed's sister. But down here in the Keys, I'm more of my own person.

I drove down here after I dropped out of school. I failed math every year. But you don't need to know algebra to sing. That's what I do now, I sing at the Crystal Room at the La Dee Dah. It's the only supper club in Key West.

Lincoln and I have different moms, but I wasn't surprised when he took up with Addison Stone. Lincoln grew up in Sag Harbor, around artists. I'm five years older, so I sort of knew our dad. In fact, I'd seen Dad the hour before he drowned himself. He'd been dismal, all out of kilter for weeks, and everyone knew it.

Addison Stone had that same blank thing her eyes. Like, really intense but also spaced out. You've had to have seen it to recognize it.

"She's got a piece of Dad in her. And I didn't need to notice her wrists first," I told Lincoln.

And he said, "Maybe so, but I can save her. We couldn't save Robard, but I can save her."

"If you say so," I told him. I'm not proud to admit this, but it made me hate Addison. Just a little bit. I guess I hated the doom she dragged in, those memories she woke up in me of Robard. And I hated that she had so much power over my kid brother.

LUCY LIM: Addy told me she wasn't coming to Rhode Island for the Christmas holidays, but I was bummed when she and Lincoln decided to go to Key West, out where his sister lived. Mom and I saw Addy's mom and her O'Hare grandparents at church on Christmas. None of them had a teaspoonful of information on Addy. They didn't even know where she was. Her brother, Charlie, wasn't home for the holidays, either. He'd gone skiing with friends in New Hampshire. I never liked Addy's folks much, but I felt sorry for them on Christmas Day. These sad old people, sharing a hymnal, singing without any thread of joy in their voices.

From: **Addison Stone** <addisonstoneart@gmail.com>
Date: Dec 27 at 6:53 PM
Subject: wish you wuz here
To: Lucy Lim <lucygracelim@gmail.com>

Lulu, Key West is the freaks.
It's full of the most rando people-trees-flowers.
All the creepiest-crawliest species stretching-reaching-flying as far down the coast as they can go.

This description also includes "Stargazer Luz." That's Linc's big sister.
I am not fan-zoning this chick.
Stargazer strolls around the bungalow, blonde and burnt,
drinking green slop for her throat, and telling us about guys who come to her cabaret act and fall madly in love with her and download all her songs.

We went to see her sing last night.
I'm surprised that she's got that gig at all.
Marilyn Monroe with extra helium.

But I'm happy!! I might be catching Keys Disease. Time ain't nothing here.
All day Lincoln basks in the sun like a lizard.
I am losing hours of my life to staring at him.

His skin is already tawny.

He smells like sex and soap.

We're hardly ever apart. I swear I get sad when he leaves to go to the toilet.

This note is making any sense? I'm dwunk.

Mojitos is the Key drink of Key West & they go down a leetle 2 EZ.

We're coming back to NYC for Eve.

Gonna be the sicccest party and you need to train for it.

Fall was the big real, huh? The deep end.

I hope next year I can take a few more calm breaths.

& enjoy Enjoy ENJOY.

x!o! & I'm so glad you liked your bracelet!

Addison in Key West, courtesy of Lincoln Reed.

Gil Cheba and Addison Stone at MXP Studio opening, courtesy of Cormac Mulvaney.

VIII.
"HE'S JUST SO STICKY AND USELESS."

GIL CHEBA, a.k.a "DJ Generate": I'm the DJ at Bembe, a club lounge in Williamsburg. I was born and raised in London, and I moved to New York about five years ago, when I was eighteen. When I first met Addison that night on New Year's Eve, I'd just returned from a stint in Ibiza, where I thought I might live and DJ happily for a while. As it happened, while I was over there, I fucked myself up rather badly on X. To the point where I knew I'd have to walk away from my entire life in Ibiza, and all the people in it, if I wanted to sort myself out.

So off I popped to rehab. Ah, rehab. It saved this poor sod's life. And once I was saved, I came back to New York City only slightly worse for my time away.

I've always thought myself a lucky chap, and I quickly got some bookings at Webster Hall, and then at the downtown Hotel Quest on New Year's Eve, which had set up two events. General party in their dining lounge, and the VIP invite-only gig was up on the rooftop around the pool. They wanted me downstairs till midnight at the general party, then *zzzzp!* up the elevator to spin for the VIP set till sunrise.

Addison Stone was the first VIP I noticed. Stunning, slinky as a mongoose, wearing a frock made of some sort of aluminum foil, violet feathers in her hair. You'd have reckoned that she was "somebody" just by the way she stood in the room. But I knew who she was. Most people did. I'd spun at countless gigs, but that night was a standout crowd. And Addison was a standout in that crowd. I remember peering down from the booth at her and thinking, *You brilliant, cheeky girl, don't you just have the world at your feet?*

LUCY LIM: Addy'd invited me to tag along at this scene-y New Year's Eve party at Quest. So intimidating! So many famous people, I was blown away. Addy was at the center of everything, and she was so *on*. She was being paid to wear a metallic dress of a young new designer, Kimber Jalloh—everyone knows what a Jalloh bag is now but I'd never heard of him then.

Addy kept telling me that she got to keep the dress. She was so excited about that. Not that she could ever wear it again. It was too fragile, like tinsel! It was falling apart. "Do NOT try this at home!" was Addy's whole style that night. She had thick silver sparkle smeared on her eyes and her trademark purple with a pair of gloves she'd dyed herself, and eight-inch platforms so she was taller than all the women and most of the men. She'd stolen a bunch of long red proteas from the hotel lobby vase and was handing them out. Proteas are a mean-looking flower, long and heavy like a sword. We were having the best time, dancing and laughing and mugging it up, and she was introducing me to a zillion people. It was all so good, till Zach Frat showed up with Sophie.

GIL CHEBA: Zach's a known tosser, and of course he wouldn't arrive anywhere without being fully crewed up with his hangers-on. The one hanging on his arm that night was Sophie Kiminski, who everyone knows as a very posh party girl and not a particularly good actress. The only vaguely thing interesting about Sophie was that she'd been on and off with Lincoln. I knew it, the room knew it, and most especially Addison Stone knew it.

Straight off, I see that Zach is putting on a show, flaunting Sophie, making a spectacle of himself so that Addison will notice. It was all quite sad, actually. Alexandre—who's not a bad bloke if he's made the decision not to act completely pretentious—was attempting to keep the peace. And so were Addison's people, everyone was stepping up hard to keep Zach away from Lincoln, to keep Sophie away from Addison. Clusterfuck is what I believe the term was for that.

ERIKSON MCAVENA: Thing was, Addison didn't like a circus unless she was the ringmaster. And when pretty, wispy, tipsy, coked-up Sophie tottered in, she was certainly getting a lot of looks. It was more drama than the Kentucky derby backstretch, I'll tell you that much.

But just to put in one good word about that night—my shot of Alexandre Norton. He'd found a pair of little kids' water wings, and he'd stuck them on for fun, and I was inspired. I asked him to jump in the shallow end. I reckon he'd have done anything that night to distract Zach from Lincoln. Plus he was a little buzzed. I used the picture in my first solo show. So not all was lost.

Photograph of Alexandre Norton, courtesy of Erickson McAvena.

LUCY LIM: Look, I'd never even met Zach Frat till that night! That's how fast he'd been in and out of Addison's life. But I recognized him, and of course I knew who Sophie was. I knew how hard it was for Addy to have to deal with Sophie, who's such a mess that it almost presents itself as awesome. She's the kind of actress whose best role is playing herself as this tragic victim of her own fame, and she's got that whole blank-stare thing down pat. Addy could never be like that. Addy didn't play at being Addy. She was always hyper-real. It seemed like a cheap trick on Zach's part.

But I wouldn't have guessed how that night would roll out. I'm never on the side of the guy who throws the first punch. Not at funerals, and not at parties. I thought Lincoln was the coolest dude on the planet, right up to that second when he punched Zach in the mouth.

MARIE-CLAIRE BROYARD: It was like a crime scene. Who knew all that blood could come gushing out of a nose? There were even drops of blood on my shoes! The way I saw it, Lincoln knew that Addison was getting emotional about Sophie, and so he just *charged* at Zach. Darling, I'll always be Team Zachary; I've known him since we were seven years old and we took ballroom dancing class together. Zach's no street fighter. And that night was *horrifically* embarrassing for him.

Lincoln's known to be edgy—I mean, his art is deeply awful, don't you think? Those poisoned, gruesome people? Those apocalyptic, end-of-days visions? Though I did hear that after Addison died, Lincoln—maybe out of guilt—went on some spiritual journey, and now I hear he's re-identifying himself as a shaman. But quite honestly, I never think you lose that *core of self* that's the real you from birth. Lincoln's core is *dark*. Which is why Addison loved him. Because she had her own demons. Anyway, I thought Lincoln was nothing but a little shit that night. Violent, stupid, immature—and I told him so.

LINCOLN REED: Why'd I punch Zach? For one, I was showing off. For another, I'd trained as a boxer for years—my mom had a string of boyfriends after Robard, and one of them owned a gym in Sag. I knew I could throw a real punch. It was wrong of Zach to bring Sophie.

It destabilized Addison. It pissed me off. It made Sophie feel used. All I wanted was to ring in New Year's Eve with my girl, for God's sake. But I ended up creating more stupid drama, so my bad.

New Year's Eve, that's supposed to be a perfect night, right? In my pocket was this onyx-and-silver pendant I'd designed especially for her.

The press made Zach out to be this jackass who deserved it. But I was just as much to blame. The way the newspapers talked about that incident, I think it all contributed to Zach's behavior toward Ads afterward. So that makes me responsible, too, right? Because I was the one who cut the power on Zach's pride.

And I paid for that.

AUTHOR'S NOTE SOPHIE KIMINSKI, WHO DECLINED to be interviewed for this book, is a Canadian actress who is still best known as a regular cast member on the popular Canadian television drama *In the Soup*, where from age nine through fifteen, she played the roles of identical twins Sammy and Frankie. In recent years, her career as an actress has been eclipsed by her substance abuse problems, which have often made her the focus of tabloids and paparazzi.

MARIE-CLAIRE BROYARD: Do you want to know the other *horrendous* part of that night? New Year's Eve was also the moment that Addison found her new BFF. You know who I mean, right? Gil "DJ Generate" Cheba? Now *that* boy is a disreputable character.

ARN: You go out quite a lot, and you've become pretty friendly with some of the fixtures of New York nightlife . . . Marie-Claire Broyard, for example. And Gil Cheba. These people are known for having a certain style.

AS: I think certain artists respond to style. We all live in a swamp of influence. I'm influenced by thirty million things a day—the weather, if I ate something delicious for breakfast, a book I just read, the edgy-looking couple that I saw in the subway. But because I paint portraits, of course I'm influenced by personal style, too. Gil and Marie-Claire have a New York style that knocks me out. As do the fabulous Nortons, Alexandre and Stephanie. As do the Lutz brothers.

But I also like to paint strangers. I love that I never know who I'm going to meet next in New York. Sometimes I imagine all these millions of kids who have come here like jeweled doorknobs marked "turn me." It's an Alice-in-Wonderland kind of city.

Gil Cheba has a facial architecture that makes you want to look twice. I want to wait till I'm a better painter before I paint him. He has so many options and moods, and he exposes so much of his soul. He's an open person; he doesn't have barriers. I know people have their issues with Cheba, but if I listened to anything people ever told me about anybody, I'd be in Peace Dale, married and having babies while my soul collapsed. I just know that's true.

LUCY LIM: One night, it was sometime in January, Addy calls me from New York, and she's crying. Really sobbing.

"Somebody's trashed my studio."

"Trashed it?"

"Destroyed, Lulu."

"What? What are you talking about?" I'm shouting into the phone. I can't believe what she's telling me. I can barely understand what she's saying, she is crying so hard. Addy's not a crier. But what I finally got out of her was that someone had broken into her workspace in Chelsea and ruined everything. Her sketches, charcoals, studies, and this portrait she'd been working on, a portrait of her mother, another of Lincoln. Works she'd never inventoried, things she'd never reproduce.

"I'm sure this is Zach. Or one of Zach's hired goons," she said.

"Don't jump to conclusions, Addy."

But Addy was sure that Zach had done it as payback—and all because Lincoln had thrown that punch.

OZO FRATEPIETRO: My wife made my name famous. I myself have very little to do with the art world. Carine and I divorced several years ago. I make my home half the time in Paris, and the other half in Montepulciano. My soul is Tuscan. It is where I go to disappear.

One night, I get a call on my private phone. This private phone line, it rings maybe four times a year. It is the girl Addison Stone. I recognize her name. I know that my ex-wife is compelled by her art and thinks she is some kind of a genius. I know that she has been in a volatile relationship with my son. But I myself have never met this girl. How does she even have this number?

What Addison Stone said on the telephone about Zachary . . . these things are not repeatable or printable.

It is hard to communicate the disrespect of her diatribe. She was threatening me. Her belief was that Zachary had destroyed her artwork and her livelihood.

I hung up the phone and considered calling the police. Then I thought better. I would not stoop to her level. I am not a child.

ERICKSON MCAVENA: She was biting and snapping at everyone. I heard she even got hold of Zach's father—ha, I'd loved to have eavesdropped on that call. I've got no extra knowledge on whether Zach himself was to blame for all that monkeyshines with Addison's studio. But Addison was one hundred percent positive and bent on revenge.

Around that time, if Addison wasn't over at Lincoln's, then she'd be with Gil Cheba, either outside on the fire escape or in the shared courtyard space, so that Gil could smoke. I never let him smoke in the apartment. Or, if it was too cold, they'd be heads-to-tails on our velvet sofa, drinking some nasty cocktail they called "rummy-dums" that Gil'd brewed up on our stove. Rum, butter, cloves. Simmer for seventeen hours. They'd drink and plot. And that was no good, for Addison, since one tablespoon of rum could just about knock her sideways.

I'd come home and say, "How's the diabolical master plan to kill Zach going?"

And they'd play all innocent. "We weren't talking about Zach."

And I'd say, "That's not possible. You two are always talking about Zach."

And then they'd both look guilty as a three-dollar bill.

That month is the only example I can give from Addison's life where she was wasting time. And it was all Gil Cheba. Wasting his own time, and everyone else's he could pull down with him.

Gil Cheba and Addison Stone in Brooklyn together, winter, courtesy of Erickson McAvena.

LINCOLN REED: Nothing about Gil Cheba washed right. Growing up around artists, I've seen too many of them lose to alcohol and drugs. Those anti-psychotic medications, the kind I knew Addison was on, just don't mix with recreational habits. Cheba is also known as a "connector"—somebody who can get you Cuban cigars or guns or your own personal harem.

He swore to everyone he'd cleaned up, but everything about that guy smelled like an addict to me. He could rationalize and simplify and excuse everything. It killed me that Addison was intrigued by him. She always liked the brink, and anyone who was standing on it. She knew he was dangerous. Gil was exhausting to be around, even though he didn't do anything much, he always wanted to distract himself—sex, booze, chatter, parties, music, feuds. The guy had no impulse control. But where Addison saw a charismatic renegade, all the rest of us only saw a bad seed.

ANONYMOUS: You already know I met Stone through Cheba. Me and Cheba, we've been buddies for years, from old days, way back. Not to get too much into the background of who I am, but what I like to say is I'm an upstanding, can-do guy working on the other side of the law. Call me a revenge handyman. I get shit done, and not for cheap.

The night we met, I liked Stone right away. She did not fool the fuck around. She says to me, first thing, "You gotta torch this house for me."

"Sure, I'll do it. For a price."

"Name it," she says.

Turned out to be a guest cottage on a piece of property out in Wainscot. That's a pretty big job, but doable.

Stone said, "I've got the cash." She was not intimidated, this one. She wasn't a pushover. She wanted to video-record the whole thing, too. When I said that'd cost extra, she told me, "I've got all the extra you need." It was a risk. But yeah, I did it. Pretty clean job, in the end.

ZACH FRATEPIETRO: Look, I can only go into this so deep. Our family has been advised not to get into conversations about Cloud Walk, since we're working on a settlement with Addison's estate. But I got that call at about 2 A.M. from my mother. Who got the call from our groundskeeper, the police department, and the fire department.

Treetops Cottage was one of three guest houses at Cloud Walk—that's our family estate in the Hamptons. It had been burnt to a crisp. Arson. Nobody was there at the time. I knew who'd done it. We all did.

The funny thing is that I knew I wouldn't press charges. I might have made threats, but burning down that house was Addison's demented love letter to me. You want to know something I never told anybody? Treetops was the very same cottage where Addison and I had stayed for a weekend last summer, over the Fourth of July weekend. The place was symbolic to her.

MARIE-CLAIRE BROYARD: The whole game of *escalating* revenge between Addison and Zach was crucial for Zach. It was the way he could stay in Addison's life. In contrast, Addison was excited by the by-product of her revenge, which was performance art. I'm sure she also enjoyed the spectacle of burning down Zach's family's property. It was interesting, brutal, destructive, dramatic—and not much to do with Zach at all.

But Zach couldn't see it that way. He took her rage personally. He saw their feud as a way to keep Addison close to him. The way a naughty child doesn't mind what kind of attention he gets, as long as he's getting it. In this sad, sick way, he *loved* that Addison smoked the guest cottage. He thought it meant he mattered.

From: **Addison Stone** <addisonstoneart@gmail.com>
Date: Jan 29 at 1:29 AM
Subject: further to ZF
To: Lucy Lim <lucygracelim@gmail.com>

You know what it is, Lulu?
I never expected that cool-as-a-martini Zach Frat would be so stupid & useless.
I thought he'd go away quietly.
Thought he'd stop thinking about me right when I stopped thinking about him.

At precisely the moment I did.

Which was unrealistic and possibly flat-out dumb
and maybe even cruel of me.
I never understood how deep he went with me.
How lost he was without me.

Not until he began all his reindeer games.
Now I hardly remember when or what was good between us.
It's just cat and mouse. All I'm doing is waiting
Wondering, watching my back.
He'll nail me for arson, maybe. If he finds the fingers that are pointing
back to me.
All I can tell you, I hope he doesn't think this game
has any rules.

Because it doesn't.

Addison and Lincoln at Kolber Gallery, courtesy of Kolber Gallery.

IX.

"I'M BLOOMING, FINALLY."

ERICKSON MCAVENA: Our lease was up in August. By February, Teddy was spending most of his time on Court Street, and Addison was usually at Lincoln's place in Soho. So the obvious future was for her and Lincoln to feather their own love nest, and for Teddy to take over Addison's rent. Addison and Lincoln were stupid for each other those days, besides.

"You remind me of a pair of baby orangutans," I used to tell them.

Just the way they'd sit on the couch, her legs flung over him, her fingers in his hair, and he'd be nuzzling her neck—this wreck of limbs, like they might start picking mites off each other's skin or digging their fingers up each other's noses any minute. They only wanted to breathe each other's oxygen.

Was I the only person who could feel this dust storm of doom kicking up around her? Addison was giving the world her story of a shiny-eyed artist in the big city. But if you scratched that surface, you had a wild kid zooming around in too many directions. Here was a girl who'd just *hired an arsonist*. A girl who'd dropped all her spring classes and who wouldn't even be getting her GED. A girl who never saw what was wrong with stealing—in fact, who felt a kind of Robin Hood ethical rightness in theft.

I liked to think I was good peeps for Addison. But Max Berger, Gil Cheba, even Marie-Claire—this wasn't always a thoughtful posse. Addison could get confused about the candy-ass image of a person versus the hard truth. She'd made that mistake with Zach. She'd made that mistake with Berger. And now here she was caught up in Cheba's whole "I've been to the edge" British bad-boy thing. What they'd say down South about Addison is she was a girl who could get her head turned too easy.

I kept on her about the five-finger discounts. The Bergdorf prank had made her bold. But the claw-foot bathtub was over the top, even for her.

"You're dumber than a sack of hammers," I'd tell her.

"Heists are fun," she'd answer. "They take my mind off my problems. Whoever is dumb enough to buy that tub is dumb enough to buy it again."

"Yeah, but this is about you. And one day, you'll get caught," I warned, "and there won't be any Max Berger to do the damage control so that you come off all cute and respectable in *Mirror Mirror*."

She wasn't listening. She never listened.

MARIE-CLAIRE BROYARD: Did you know Addison and Gil dressed up as FedEx workers to steal the tub? Once she had it, she had it hauled the five flights up to the Court Street apartment, then filled it with plantings—forsythia bushes and a mulberry tree. It looked wonderful.

The tub's *still* at that old apartment. It's too heavy to move. Here's something sentimental—I went into Brooklyn just the other week to see it. Kind of a pilgrimage, to the old apartment where so much of Addison's spirit is contained. The tub is right where it always was, in front of the living room window and still filled with greens.

"Addison Stone *stole* that tub," I told the couple who are renting there now. They just about lost their *minds*, they thought it was so fabulous.

MAXWELL BERGER: These mind games—Zach Frat destroying Addison's sketches, Addison burning down his guest cottage in the Hamptons—they might have been selling copies of *The New York Post*, but they weren't helping Addison's career.

I called her. I never make calls, but I called her. I said, "You get your act together. You're disappearing onto the front page. Commercial is one thing. Flame-out's another."

ARLENE FIELDBENDER: Addison and I met for lunch in late January. I took off from teaching especially to come down and see her. By then, she'd dropped all her art classes for that spring semester. I hadn't given her any push-back when she decided to stop the general curriculum. But the art classes? That was shortsighted to the point of stupidity, and I told her so.

We met at her studio. I saw the finished *Doc* and some of her studies that would be *Exit Roy*. And I saw some sketches for her self-portrait. Her portrait work was leaning more deeply to abstraction, and she was working in watercolor. The work was emotional and poignant, though I noticed she was discarding a lot of it. Most of her studies in butcher-block paper, she'd made big slashing black *X*s through the faces. She was too quick to edit and negate. Too hard on herself, I thought.

Addison herself was a little off, as well. She was bouncing in too many directions. During lunch at a coffee shop around the corner from her studio, she gushed all about how she was in love with Lincoln Reed. How she couldn't live without him. How he was everything to her. But then in the next second, she'd flash to anger. Zach had destroyed her studio. Zach was out to get her. She went through an itemization of all that she'd lost.

Her brain then seemed to spiral naturally to the Coulsen article. I admit it was unsettling. Addison was always a mile a minute, but throughout the lunch, she couldn't seem to stay on point in conversation. I was concerned that she might need more intensive psychiatric help. A reassessment. I came back to Peace Dale and told Bill I was a bit worried that Addison was losing her grip on her future. She seemed overly distracted by relationships.

But then, of course, the Whitney came knocking.

DR. ROLAND JONES: Until those last weeks, the last weeks of her life, Addison was very good about appointments. She'd spent some of them working on a painting of me. A wonderful portrait, if only I could have afforded it, ha! So I got to know her both as a client and an artist. Over that winter into spring, she was busy, industrious, but, no—I didn't feel that Addison was overwhelmed by any one aspect of her life.

In particular, she always spoke of Lincoln Reed in an upbeat manner. She called him her "soul mate" and said that she "had never known and been known as well by another person." She'd mention his healthy habits—how he ran and biked, that he vehemently abstained from drinking, and that he liked to get to sleep at a reasonable hour. So when she informed me that they were moving in together, this seemed—from my professional point of view—a positive thing.

She also told me that she'd been trying to break a bad habit of slashing her paintings. She confessed she'd often strike a red or black *X* through a piece if it wasn't working the way she wanted. Apparently, Lincoln had spoken up numerous times against this act. He called it sabotage, a vandalism against herself. He thought she gave up too easily. He seemed to be sensitive to her self-destructive impulses in general.

Doc, a painting of Roland Jones, by Addison Stone, courtesy of the Deutsche Bank private collection.

LUCY LIM: Moving in with Lincoln was a huge mistake. I love Lincoln dearly, but Addy never, ever should have done it. He wanted to rescue her. He wanted to try. She hated to be alone. But no matter how vulnerable Addy felt about the whacked-out games Zach was playing, no matter how insecure she felt about the Coulsen article, no matter how much she said Lincoln Reed made her feel loved and safe . . . those two artists—too much together, too soon after meeting—equaled Very Bad Idea.

She begged me to come visit during a face-bitingly cold weekend, right after she moved in with him. She paid for my train ticket on the Acela and then a private town car from Penn Station to downtown, the usual Addison treatment. The Fieldbenders had also asked if I would please report back, and so I knew they were worried, too.

Lincoln lived on Elizabeth Street, smack in the chic heart of Soho. The freight elevator opened up right into his raw living space—it must have been two thousand square feet. Addy loved all that space and light—she was like a kid, showing me how the door to the bedroom slid sidewise like in a barn. She loved the concrete floor, the industrial cool, and of course those strangely hypnotizing Lincoln Reed canvases propped all along the walls.

But I think a lot of Addy's identity got left behind on Court Street. She'd painted her purple walls with such joy. The tub was back there, plus other things people had legit given her—Marie-Claire, for one, had delivered Addy a life-sized stuffed rhinoceros from FAO Schwartz. The Lenox had sent her a tree stump from Colorado, with the bark polished to sable. Those were her own special things, and they were part of her story. But Addy insisted that she didn't care about any of that, and she didn't want to take anything but bare essentials to Lincoln's.

"I like thinking about The Queen's Shame looking exactly the same," she said. "That place is like an art installation of my past. I don't want to tamper with it."

Lincoln didn't believe in clutter or possessions. Addy wanted to play along. But Addy, a girl who could create some of the most beautiful things I'd ever seen, never really owned anything valuable or interesting till New York. Typical Addy, she just walked away from it all. Maybe she had a point. Maybe the only thing of value in an Addy-charged environment was Addy.

Elizabeth Street was Lincoln's territory. Starting with his artwork and ending with his artwork, because Lincoln painted in the same place where he lived. His canvases were everywhere. Addy's workplace was up in Chelsea. So none of her prints or paints or in-progress work were at home. But she didn't want to bring anything to Lincoln's space, either.

"I'd rather get lost in Lincoln's brain," she told me once. "I want to come back from my studio and forget about myself for a while. Soak him in."

I didn't ask her if she missed Erickson, but I did. Erickson was a different roomie groove than Lincoln. He's a laid-back, sweet presence. His and Teddy's love is a big hug that invites you in and warms you up. Plus Erickson is a natural host. When I'd come visit on Court Street, Erickson would always whip up his Southern specialties, like fried zebra tomatoes with deviled eggs and sweet hibiscus tea.

Lincoln is the opposite. An absentminded-professor type. That guy can't even boil water. And from what I could tell, he's always been a loner.

"You want to rescue her," I said to Lincoln when Addy was in the bathroom, and we had a brief moment alone. "I get it. But she's a full-time job. She was my job, and then she was Erickson's, and now she's yours. And you never saw what happened last time, when Zach tried to take over that job."

"I won't fuck it up, Lucy," he said. "I promise."

I looked into his eyes and knew he meant it. But I also knew he couldn't possibly have understood what he was getting into.

Lincoln Reed, parking his bike in his studio on Elizabeth Street, courtesy of Lucy Lim.

ERIKSON MCAVENA: Oh, yeah, I was incredibly depressed when she left. Sure, it was fun to start playing house with Teddy. At this point, we're like a pair of old socks. We've been together so long, almost seven years now. But it had been barely six months I'd lived with Addison. And then she was gone.

The good news was we'd always meet for brunch at this great breakfast place, Cafeteria, after I was done with my 10 A.M. photography class in Union Square. We'd get johnny-cake and cheddar grits and a giant pot of coffee, and we'd catch up.

One morning she came in looking kinda dazed. Her hair in braids, too, which always meant she was prickly.

"I've been up most of the night," she told me. "You'll never guess. I've been sent a message in a dream. The message was from Willem de Kooning. We were riding the elevator together, and he said the strangest thing to me. He said, 'Claim what is valuable. Take back what's yours.'"

First I thought this was Addison's ass-backward way of telling me she wanted everything she'd left behind at The Queen's Shame. Then I thought she was messing with me. So I started making fun.

"Sugar," I said, "I didn't know de Kooning talked like the Oracle in *The Matrix*."

"No no no, I'm serious, Erickson. Don't you get it?" Those dark bright eyes on me. "De Kooning has given me my first truly epic idea. I'm ready for it, too. I'm blooming, finally."

"I think you need a second opinion," I told her.

But she wasn't listening. She'd already decided what this dream meant, and if I didn't get it, she didn't care.

LINCOLN REED: No, I didn't understand the de Kooning dream at first. When she explained her interpretation of it, I thought she was kidding. Because she had somehow decided, from this one little dream, that de Kooning had appeared to her to tell her to steal her portrait out of the Whitney.

"I'd be very careful with this concept," I told her. "It's one thing to sneak a few fancy dresses out of Bergdorf's, or even FedEx-deliver yourself a bathtub. But to attempt to illegally remove your own art from a famous museum? Why would you bite the hand that's feeding you? And why risk being arrested, and having that on your record?"

"No, no, Linc," she answered, "I'm *replacing* the portrait in the Whitney with a video of me stealing me. I'm taking back what's mine. I'm claiming what is valuable. I'm swapping one art form for another. So everyone will come away happy. Best possible outcome."

I said, "Jail is also a possible outcome."

ADDISON STONE (from her own recorded notes): I'm moving ahead with this project. De Kooning knew better than anyone how artists need to be in constant metamorphosis. We make something, and we want the world to see it, but then we want to make it all over again, with a new skewering. Which reminded me of that Emily Dickinson quote that English teachers love too much: "tell all the truth but tell it slant." Because your truth, your way, is always slant. And I think I could make my slant amazing. I want to be my own curator, to give with one hand and grab with the other. Now that I've been handed this idea, I'll do everything in my power to execute it.

DOMINICK LUTZ: Addison was a straight-up adrenaline junkie. She disguised her junkie need by calling it art. But. When she came to me with this objective—to steal her own self-portrait, the only self-portrait she'd ever done, out of the Whitney, and then swap in a video of herself performing this magic trick, I had to say, "Well, fuck yeah. Let me in." I thought it was so pure, so courageous. It made me think about—*What is theft?* What's this act that is defined as "theft" when you're stealing the property you yourself created? Is it a felony? Is it art?

I didn't know. I didn't care.

CAMERON LUTZ: Getting on board with Addison's vision took me a while. Okay, it took me a whole night out with Addison and Lincoln and Paloma and Dom. In the end, I agreed. I was—still *am*—the cautious brother. I'm also the tech brother. So it was up to me to learn about the security system in the Whitney. We ended up calling the whole job Project #53, because that was Addison's placement in the show, hers the fifty-third piece of art. That number was how Addison's work appeared in all the security blueprints and maps. If I live to be a hundred, and I need to bullet the top ten most incredible things that I ever did, Project #53 would be—bam—right at the top of that timeline.

LUCY LIM: Addison was calling me a lot around then. She didn't write me emails. She was paranoid that Zach was paying spies and moles at Bing and Yahoo and Google to report all her activity back to him. But she'd call to talk through Project #53. How the Lutz brothers were going to master the technical aspects. Sometimes she spoke about the general risk aspects—she sometimes worried about how they might all get caught, and what the punishment would be.

Mostly she was on a high from the idea.

"Finally, Lu!" Practically screaming it into the phone. "Finally, Lu! Finally!" So sincere, I'd never have the heart to pop her balloon. I mean, *finally*? She'd been in New York for less than a year!

But for the very first time, my gut told me she wasn't taking the best care of herself. "Don't forget, Addy. An apple a day keeps Glencoe away."

"Not if it's Snow White's apple," she answered.

"Ha ha ha. Keep eating right, and take your Z," I'd always say it jokingly, casually. But I was also creeping around online, reading up on antipsychotic medications, hoping Jones and Tuttnauer and the Fieldbenders were listening to Addy as hard as I was.

Lincoln also called me a few times, because he suspected that Addy had been self-weaning onto a lower dosage. Lincoln said that Addison often spoke about wanting to "get clean," a.k.a. off Z completely. And he told me she was definitely borrowing some of his regime, not skipping meals, getting her sleep, taking Citi Bike. She felt good and strong, and she hated that her personality was being filtered through an anti-psychotic medication. Getting off Z would be the last step to health.

One thing that can be true of people with Addy's exact mental health problems is they think if they're happy and busy and the sun is out and life is smiling on them, then why do they need this little pill? So they think maybe the pill's got nothing to do with it. Maybe, hallelujah, they're cured? Then they go off the pill on the DL, and they're back in the storm with their demons before anyone knew they'd wandered off. The other downside is that once you ease off a medication like Zyprexa, there's no assurance it stays the right key to lock those demons back up and get you out safe.

All to say, I wanted Project #53 to be over and done with.

MAXWELL BERGER: Project #53. Did I know about it? No. Did not. Not until it happened. Not until I read it in the headlines. When I saw Addison, at various galleries and shows, she'd give me her usual earful. She'd never forgiven me for the *Mirror Mirror* piece, which had come out in February. Although frankly, I'd thought it had been very good for her brand. But she disrespectfully disagreed.

Addison caught in conversation with Max Berger at the Joaquin Capa exhibit, spring, courtesy of Kate Volkmann.

MARIE-CLAIRE BROYARD: Well, she wasn't going out as much—not at night, certainly, but not much by day, either. Over that winter, we used to have these fun "Red Door" afternoons, where I'd scoop Addison off to Elizabeth Arden and pummel her into a manicure and brow wax and facials. General maintenance! Skin gets so dry in winter, dearie.

But Addison dropped her nightlife and her spa days, too, when she sank into Project #53. Addison had always been a girl you could count on to stay out until the wee hours, every night of the week. And somehow she'd be fresh as a daisy tomorrow.

So one afternoon, I wanted to see how fresh she was when she *didn't* go out all night. I stopped by Lincoln's place, only to find out that Addison had just about taken it over *completely*.

"Check it out, Marie-Claire. My floor plans of the Whitney. I'm using this to recreate the space where my portrait is hanging. This is how we're choreographing the film—don't mind the mess!"

"Mess? That's an understatement, Addison. You're living in *squalor*," I told her. "And you're dragging poor Lincoln down with you."

"Oh, please. You're overreacting," she told me.

"Marie-Claire's just reacting," Lincoln shouted over. Laughing it off.

But I'm telling you, the place was trashed. Half-eaten take-out in boxes, cans of Red Bull and bottles of vitaminwater, dirty paint smocks and notebooks, stacks of magazines, and heaps of clothing everywhere. That girl had such *horrific* habits.

Poor Lincoln was attempting to work. He was painting on the way other side of the loft—but I wondered how he could even concentrate, with so much Addison-osity sucking up the oxygen. And I also remember that Addison, uncharacteristically, didn't seem to care much about what Lincoln was up to. It was as if something had shifted inside her. She was *brimming* with her own plans. I was curious about what Lincoln thought of all that disorder in his home—but he seemed quite sweet and good-boyfriend-supportive. So I kept my trap shut.

LINCOLN REED: She went deep. Really deep. She dropped Cheba for a while, which I appreciated. But she also got that heinous tattoo, which I didn't appreciate.

LUCY LIM: There are things I wish I could do over. And telling Addison about Ida is one of them. At the time, right after she'd moved into Lincoln's, I hadn't considered how that information would affect her. But now, with the rest of my life to reflect on it, I have to wonder.

Over that winter break, I'd hunted down Ida. I'd been sleuthing, and finally, I found a name in a census poll, right outside Bristol in Dartmouth. Ida Grimes, 1899 to 1919. Dead by twenty. I didn't have much else. No photograph, no cause of death. But I'd placed an Ida in Dartmouth, and that seemed worth mentioning to Addy.

So I did. I thought it would validate something for her, the way it had for me. Like, make her realize maybe it wasn't all cooked up by mental illness? But why had I just assumed "Ida Grimes" would give Addy peace? Maybe because I'd always hated to think that she'd invented Ida. A poltergeist seemed so harmless, compared with all of those sharpened blades inside Addy's own head.

What I didn't know was that instead of closing Pandora's box, it broke the lid off. Maybe it would have come off, anyway. But sometime that spring, Addy got someone at Sacred Tattoo to ink Ida's name and dates to the back of her neck. I didn't see it till spring break. By then, of course, I totally regretted I'd said anything.

LINCOLN REED: Lucy came to me with all her Ida guilt around the same time Addison had started Project #53. She's such a good soul, and always alert to shifts in Addison's moods. And Lucy was as good a friend to me as she was to Addison. We could text each other jokes, ways to share and shrug off our fears. When Lucy and I talked through anything Addison— her manic swings, her talent, her stunts, her heists, her random acts of tattoo—I felt straightened out. I could deal with Addison, as long as I had Lucy's advice ringing in my ears.

LUCY LIM: Basically, I said to Lincoln, "Act like you're happy she did it. Tell Addy that you see the Ida Grimes tattoo as a way of her making peace with Ida. Pretend you think this is Addy's way of accepting that Ida Grimes is a guardian angel or a muse." That was the baloney I was feeding myself, anyway.

DR. ROLAND JONES: No. I didn't know about what she had tattooed onto the back of her neck. She kept that hidden from me. As a matter of fact, beginning with that spring and Project #53, Addison kept quite a lot hidden from me.

LINCOLN REED: The tattoo wasn't a stand-alone gesture. Addison's reach was competing with her grasp to get to Project #53. She got very spiritual and monkish that whole week before the big event, which was March 15, the Ides.

We decided to prep for it together. Which started out corny —but then turned serious. We created an ashram out of the loft. We decided not to speak out loud. No email, phone or texts, not that Addison had any presence online. She didn't keep a Facebook account or Twitter or Tumblr. She thought all of those things were distractions, scrapbooks that blocked and disrupted your real life. We meditated, she went cold turkey off the junk food, and we limited our intake to staples like dark greens, nuts and fruits. We listened to Gregorian chants and Steve Reich's *Music for 18 Musicians*, and we did Bikram yoga by sundown. No light except candles.

It was extreme, but I loved being in Addison's skin with her—she was so purposeful and single-minded about #53.

She had created their Whitney blueprint design on vellum paper in addition to the copy on her hard drive, plus she had memorized the play-by-play she'd made with Cam and Dom. It showed everything that needed to go down once the Whitney's alarm system was suspended. We studied it every night, the last thing we did before we went to bed.

That entire week we slept facing each other. Same breath, same pulse.

"Synchronicity empowers me," Addison told me. She even wrote it on my bathroom wall, in this beautiful lettering over my medicine cabinet. I look at it every morning, though now of course, since she's been gone, the message reads very differently.

On the last morning, we woke up and realized we'd been holding hands all night. Thoughts of failure—an unsuccessful break-in, getting arrested and becoming the punch line of the next day's news, defeating her ego, destroying her reputation—we refused to think about that. We were on the tightrope, and we couldn't look down.

DOMINICK LUTZ: Addison had made a replica of the plastic-encased museum card to replace what she'd exhibited. So instead of having a card that read, *Addison Stone: Self-Portrait*, it read, *Film of the Theft of the Self-Portrait of Addison Stone*. I always loved that touch. Addison could get the details so right, from restyling her T-shirt to that last stroke of the brush that jumped an image to life. She did nothing halfway.

That night of #53, we'd set up a tripod in front of her piece. The video is simple—all you see are the white-gloved hands, like butler's hands. Cam, me, and Addison. We remove the painting from the wall and take it offscreen. Addison was supposed to replace herself. Reposition her portrait with her own face on film where the portrait had been hanging. Then five long beats, click the remote to stop the camera, boom. End.

Our plan was to leave the tripod right there, and run this on an unending loop. So instead of looking at Addison's portrait, you're watching the movie of the portrait being stolen, and the subject of the portrait take the portrait's place—as if she is sitting for her portrait.

That night, everything is clockwork. Addison did her beats. But then, after she jumped off, she whipped out a can of spray paint from her hoodie pocket and tagged, z, FUCK U on the wall. The whole thing was so immature. So beneath Addison Stone's artistry. Plus it added seven crippling seconds to the video. It was completely wrong for the flow and the meta of the film.

Cam and I came as close as we ever have to writing Addison out of our lives for that. We'd risked big. For sure, part of me is still in grudge mode. I still have dreams where I'm yelling at her. Even now. She'd dragged us into this high-art stunt, and then she turned it into a vendetta against an old boyfriend? We both felt betrayed.

LUCY LIM: Addy's mind was genius. But her heart was sometimes stuck in high school. And how can you blame her for hating Zach? Or for taking out her anger in a major public way, which was where Addy took everything? I wish she'd had more time here. Time on earth, I mean, to make truly spectacular and mature works of art. Addison never grew up. She never got to become the force she ought to have been.

LINCOLN REED: Up till the moment Cam showed me the feedback loop, I'd been hugely respectful of #53. But when I saw Ads writing that message—to Zach Frat, of all people—I felt sick. So wrong. First I felt like Addison had stepped into dog shit as an artist. Second, I felt that she'd screwed our relationship. My usual reaction to a situation I can't process was just to bolt. So I did.

STARGAZER LUZ: My brother drove straight from New York to see me in Key West. All the way down the East Coast. It took him a day and a night, and he pulled in around 3 A.M. We sat in my kitchen, and he spilled his heart. He talked about how much he loved Addison Stone, and about how he couldn't deal with her—her careless habits, her demands, the emotional space she sucked out of his private life. He told me how he hated Gil Cheba and Zach Frat and Max Berger. He told me how her mania unnerved him. He told me he was debilitated to think he'd never know a love as big as his and Addison's. At the same time, even the love felt like too much.

But mostly he talked about what Addison did at the Whitney. He couldn't believe that after all the prep work, and all the conversations, the soul-searching, and all the deep thinking that Addison put into this project, that she'd gone and made it into a Zach-revenge thing.

At one point, Addison sent him a photo of what she'd done to her self-portrait. She'd blurred the eyes and mouth. *"My Face Is Tears,"* she wrote him. "Come back to me."

I advised him not to. Nobody knows what it's like to live with a ticking time bomb unless you've done it before. Mom and I'd lived that way with Robard. And it was awful. Truly damaging.

My Face Is Tears by Addison Stone, courtesy of The Sinclair Corp.

MAXWELL BERGER: "Art Babe Takes Self, Leaves Proof." It's a killer headline, the one in *The Times*. Big, honking scandal. I couldn't have scripted it better, except for the bullshit at the end. But I got that changed, got Zach Frat excised. The next day I had my people scrub the video, so that it could be what it was meant to be. Addison knew we'd get techies to trim it. So nobody who saw the Biennial ever saw Zach. And as everyone knows, Addison was the hit of the show.

ERICKSON MCAVENA: Now that Addison's gone, and there's a basic agreement that the arts lost another genius, there's also a conversation out there about the lasting significance of her work. I'm real pleased for that. But when she was alive, a lot of people treated her mostly as a curiosity—a high-stepping, three-legged show-pony. You can take Max Berger to task for a lot, but he always knew she was major. The fact that she's so big now, revered, so soon after her death—I'm not sure if it would have made her laugh or pissed her off.

ZACH FRATEPIETRO: In the end, if you cracked open everything that was Addison, and spread out all of those different parts of her life in front of you, the machine always builds and rebuilds to create an Addison-and-Zach monster. That's all I'm saying about #53.

BILL FIELDBENDER: While Addison was thinking up Project #53, we knew she'd been working on a few other portraits. She Skyped with Arlene and me when she finished *Exit Roy*, and Max Berger sold her self-portrait, too—her careful disfiguring of her eyes and mouth had given it an extra measure of notoriety.

She'd also, very quietly, been doing some studies of Sophie

Kiminski. She had alluded to the Sophie studies once or twice, but she was always so self-critical about her early sketches that, until a finished piece emerged, it was best to assume that she was slashing Xs and discarding most of this effort.

Arlene and I really liked the finished *Exit Roy* as an example of a certain style of painting Addison was exploring. There's such deep psychological insight in this image. Her father looks washed away, uncertain, absent. As if everything he'd ever wanted to become had been siphoned out of him.

Exit Roy by Addison Stone, courtesy of Saatchi Gallery.

LUCY LIM: I saw the sketches of Sophie. She showed them to me secretly. They were really good, but kind of a shocker. Addy absolutely did not want Lincoln to find out. Everyone knew Sophie had a coke problem, and Lincoln hadn't been able to get Sophie clean, and Addy kept imagining and re-imagining Sophie all coked-up and spooky. When Addy sent me some snaps, I just about fell over. I advised her to bury the whole concept.

"The thing is, Max wants me to finish a Sophie portrait," she told me on one of our calls. "He says there's already a buyer."

"No, Addy. Don't put it out there," I said. "Lincoln and Sophie had a past. He doesn't want to be reminded. You'll hurt him."

"What about my hurt? Sophie's always talking to people about how I don't deserve Lincoln. How I'm overrated."

"She's troubled. Rise above it, Addy."

But Addison didn't like to compromise her interests. For many reasons, Sophie Kiminski was such a forbidden fruit. Addison couldn't resist.

After the Whitney, I think Addy could have sneezed into a tissue and sold it. But I knew she was following Sophie's big mouth in the press, and we all read in the tabloids how Sophie had checked into rehab for her coke habit, and Addy had on good account—Gil Cheba was friends with some friends of Sophie's—that Sophie had big plans to get Lincoln back once she'd cleaned up. This only fueled Addy's interest in capturing and owning Sophie through her art. I don't think Addy had expected how annoyed Lincoln would be.

"What do you accomplish by obsessively painting my ex-girlfriend?" he'd ask. "It's not the art you should be doing. It's creepy and sensationalist."

She'd call me and tell me about these arguments they'd have, and of course I was always sensitive to Addison's point of view, but I have to admit, I sided with Lincoln. A million portraits to paint, and she's painting vapid, wasted Sophie? Why go and stir that pot?

LINCOLN REED: Finally, it got to the point where Ads swore she wasn't working on a finished piece, but I knew that she secretly was. It depressed me that I had to hear about it through the gossip mill. And later, I found out that Berger Galleries sold the painting quick and dirty, in a private sale to an undisclosed buyer for an undisclosed amount. Obviously, Addison tried to keep the work, and the final-price sale, from me. She thought it would hurt me. She was right.

When I reassessed the relationship, the short story was that in a span of a few short months, Addison'd moved into my place, trashed it while creating Project #53, made sure that everyone remembered #53 as a Zach Frat moment, snuck off to her Chelsea studio to paint disturbing portraits of my ex-girlfriend—who at that time was apparently dating Zach—and then sold one of these portraits to a private collector through her dealer and got everyone to lie about it to me.

Soon after #53, the last weekend in March, I was doing a *Face the Nation* program in Washington. It was part of a panel on war tactics. Some of my pieces about chemical warfare were getting well-reviewed. Also, one of my half brothers was serving in Iraq. I guess the wonks thought I'd have something to say about chemical warfare, and its place in our history and our now.

Going on journalism television was a serious performance for me. Just like the Whitney had been for Ads. But where I'd been there for her, to help her, Addison was only a source of stress for me. Once I started thinking about her as harmful, almost a poison, my own personal relationship toxin, well, I couldn't unthink it.

No matter how much I loved Addison, I didn't want to keep breathing her in. Not when I could feel all the negative effects on me every day. I felt that she was crushing me, negating my space in the world. I had to let her go.

Addison leaving her apartment on 68 Front Street, Brooklyn, NY, by Sam Jeffrey for *New York Daily News*.

X.
THE JOY DIZZIES

MAXWELL BERGER: Addison came to me that spring. Must have been late April. She'd never done that before, never visited my office. But after she'd sold *Exit Roy*, she dropped by personally to pick up the check—the fattest check our accounting division had ever cut for her. She'd moved out of Lincoln's place and was renting-to-own an apartment on Front Street where all the kids were living, in DUMBO— Down Under the Manhattan Bridge Overpass. So she was back in Brooklyn, which seemed better for her. I was glad to give her the money. 'Course I had to take a chunk. But there were all the expected legal issues with the Whitney stunt, and so all of the lawyers and consulting fees would have to come out of the profit. That's the way the game is played.

Addison had been depressed. It wasn't a trade secret that the split with Lincoln Reed was the reason, but I don't get my nose in people's personal lives. These young artists, they're always sexed up, screwing this one and screwing over that one. I can't keep track, and I don't want to. But when Addison came strutting into my office with that puss on her face, I knew she'd bite my head off if I asked her what was the story.

I gave her a bottle of champagne to celebrate the sale. Just pretending along like everything was hunky-dory. Her chin was up, and her armor was on.

What do I recall most of that meeting? The last time I saw Addison? I remember she had on more airs than the Queen of England. I remember that she was sitting across from my desk, asking me about future sales and commissions. I could feel that she had her same bad taste in her mouth for me. She was interrogating me. But I didn't mind. I've been in this business a lot of years. Addison was a one-of-a-kind talent. Hey, I was glad she wanted to know. Sometimes it's good to peek inside the factory and see how the sausage gets made.

I did say something to her, toward the end of our powwow. "Addison, kid," I said, "you've got everything on God's green earth to look forward to. You shouldn't let these little shits, Zach or Lincoln or any of 'em, ruin all the things you're working for. Get greedy. Get greedy for yourself. That's who's gonna pull you through the hard times. Rescue yourself, and the rest will follow."

And she stared at me, it must have been a full fifteen seconds, before she said the last words I ever heard out of her mouth, "Berger, you know what? You talk a good game, but you're just like every other scumbag I ever met in New York. I don't need you to tell me how to get greedy when you're part of my whole fucking problem."

And she stood up, and she snapped up the check, stuck the bottle of champagne in her backpack, and she left. Of course, when I sold *Bloody Sophie*, the money was triple what she got for *Exit Roy*. To this day, *Bloody Sophie* is probably her most valuable piece.

LUCY LIM: When Lincoln had asked Addy to move out of the Elizabeth Street loft, *devastated* didn't even begin to describe her. She was shipwrecked. I was angry with him, sure, but could I blame him? Not in my heart. She'd become impossible to live with. But losing Lincoln took all the wind out of her.

Right afterward, Addy heard a rumor—false, it turned out—that Lincoln was seeing Sophie again. She also believed that after #53, Zach was using all his power and pulling every string he could to get her blacklisted from the scene. She assumed that he was asking for her to be banned at power parties and dropped off high-end invitations to openings and events. I have no idea if any of that was true, but in different ways, both of her exes were pulling her apart.

"Come home to Peace Dale for a while, Addy," I'd tell her on the phone. "What's prettier than a New England spring?"

"I don't have the time," she'd say. "I've got too much work."

"You're burning yourself out," I'd argue. "Your mom wants to see you. And you need to rest. At least if you're in Rhode Island, you know that you're not missing anything. There's nothing to miss."

The problem was, she never wanted to rest.

Then, I swear it was the first truly perfect pink-and-white day of spring, Addy found that place on Front Street. She sent her mom and my mom and me all the images, with these emoji hearts and smiles and captions like "maple-stained hardwood floors" and "big shower space" and "skyline!" And suddenly she seemed very grown-up. DUMBO was exactly her neighborhood, chock-full of up-and-comers, and she'd fallen in love with it. She'd made that money off *Exit Roy*, and she wanted to show she was a success. Or that cool things really can come out from dead-end romances and heartbreaking breakups.

ERICKSON MCAVENA: I was the one who helped Addison get on the stick and move herself out of Lincoln's.

"Will you come move me out, and wipe my nose when I cry?" she asked.

"I'll even bring the hankies," I told her.

When I arrived on her doorstep on move-in morning, instead of a U-Haul truck, there's only a cab outside. The girl owned nothing.

"For all the crapola you like to steal, you don't have jack squat," I teased her. Seriously, she had a couple of suitcases, a couple of boxes. The end.

Me and Teddy actually did rent a U-Haul a day later, and we brought her everything she'd left on Court Street. From her ugly sunburst coffee mugs to her stuffed rhino and even the velvet sofa. The tub stayed. That thing was too goddamn heavy, and about as useful as a trapdoor on a canoe.

Underneath, I guess I felt all kinds of guilty. Addison wanted to move back to Court Street. She'd crashed there the first weekend after the Lincoln breakup. But by then Teddy was moved in, snug as a bug. Plus we had a Craigslist tenant, MaryKate Harrington, who wasn't any Addison, but she was going to Fashion Institute of Technology, and she was paying us a pretty good rent. We couldn't just dump MaryKate a month into it. Addison knew it, but she still begged pretty hard.

"Just please let me stay there for a month or two."

"Sugar, there's cozy. And then there's the sardine tin," I told her.

"I know, I know." Then in a joking way, but kind of wistful, she said, "Maybe I could sleep on the fire escape? We could put a tin roof up. I wouldn't bother anybody."

She slayed me. I was real sorry I couldn't give her that room back. I felt lower than a worm about it. So I was relieved that Addison seemed knee-deep in clover about her new digs. It had a bathroom like the Bel Air. I guess it was around that time that Addison decided to stop working at the Chelsea studio, too. She wanted to live and work in the same space. A good call, I thought.

Move-in day, early June, was my only time I ever spent at her new place on Front Street. Teddy and I were never in that apartment again. So I don't know how she changed it up, or if she ever made it her own, the way we'd been talking about it. But that night, after we'd hauled and unpacked, the three of us ate a picnic on the floor. It was a French-style dinner, with a bottle of wine and some cheese and bread.

"Turn this space into your home, Addison," said Teddy. "Buy some lamps and rugs. Get a fricking goldfish."

Addison Stone in her Front Street apartment, courtesy of Lucy Lim.

"Or maybe I'll just steal two big-ass Barcaloungers right off the showroom floor of JCPenney. Along with a flatscreen and shag carpeting," she answered. "And heist some art from the Whitney."

When we finally left, Addison looked as lonely as the last pea at pea-time. I was relieved Lucy Lim was coming down for a few days the next week. But it was hard to say goodbye to Addison. For a moment, I guess I experienced a sense of doom. It was so unbearable. Teddy says it was a premonition. I don't know. I should have let her come back to Court Street. I should have been the one to sleep on the fire escape. She wasn't ready to live all by herself. I knew it. Everyone knew it.

LUCY LIM: I've probably spent a thousand hours thinking back on that last time I went down to New York. Looking for the signs. Combing for any clue I might have missed. The plan began lightheartedly enough. Exam week is a joke for seniors. So that's why I decided to spend some real time with Addy in the city, from Wednesday through Sunday. To check in on her, see how she was really doing in 3D.

"I'll help you settle in," I said. "We'll paint your walls."

"Oh, fun! Slumber party! We'll wear pajamas and jump on my new bed."

Even Mom wanted me to take that time off from school. What I can say for sure was that Addy was trying, but she wasn't quite herself. And by trying, I mean that she was working to stay connected. She'd stocked up on my favorite foods. She'd bought me a fluffy robe and towels and all these sweet hotel-y guest things. She asked questions about family and friends. She listened to the answers. We went on walks and hung out in coffee shops and talked and talked.

We also went out, to all these exclusive parties, and I knew she was making a giant effort to get out of her head, but also not to talk about how much she missed Lincoln, or how paranoid she was that Zach was back-stabbing her and black-listing her from all of New York. She'd picked up smoking, and she was a touch thin, which unsettled me, but something else going on with her. A restless energy, an impatience in the way she'd pick up a fork or swipe her Metro card. But I couldn't quite put my finger on it.

"Addy, are you off your Z?" I asked her, just once.

"What? No way," she promised.

"Okay, but what's up with the cigarettes?" I asked.

"It takes away my jitters," she answered.

I still counted out of her bottle in the medicine cabinet every night. But I couldn't depend on that as proof. Addy'd have known that I'd count the pills, and she'd have dropped one in the toilet every bit as routinely. I was also concerned about the creative output. She seemed a touch manic. Canvases everywhere, mostly sketches and studies for her new thing, *Bridge Kiss*, taped up.

She'd also taken to writing on the walls. Again, it seemed restless. All of these names of artists, with quotes, as well as questions to herself from herself. I remember a few, like, "Why do you use the human face?" "Do you think of your art as mainstream or outsider?" "What is your role as a painter, as a young person, as a female?" Scrawled everywhere in Sharpie. It was like she was her own preacher, asking herself the Big Questions. But no answers.

I remember some of the artists' names: Kiki Smith, Joan Jonas, Blek la Rat, and a dozen more at least. There were also stacks and stacks of books. Mostly art books. She kept books in the oven and her art supplies in the fridge.

We went out with Cheba a couple of nights. He struck me as perfectly fine, he never seemed drunk or high, so I officially don't believe what people say about him as her pusher—all I blamed him for was getting Addy started on those smokes. But I never saw him do one random thing; he never offered me drugs, nada.

At night, Addy never seemed particularly happy to be anywhere we went. She was always checking her phone. One time, I got nosy and searched her browser history, and I saw that all she did was cruise the Internet for Lincoln intel. Where he was, what he was up to. I didn't tease her. It seemed way too painful.

When I was packing to leave on Sunday, she came into my room, and she sat on the floor and broke down.

"I'm spinning, Lulu," she said, her voice breaking. "I'm spinning and spinning. My brain is like a big echoing train station filled with announcements I can't hear, and I'm trying to decide which trains I should board, but I can't make any decisions because it's too noisy."

"You're off it, aren't you?" I said. "Just tell me. You need to pause, Addy. You need to step away. I'll step with you. And you've got to let meds work for you. If the Z isn't working, you need to find a new protocol. You need to call your doctors, or let me call them."

But she just shrugged me off. Swore she was still on the Z, that it was still working. Waving off my words with her hand. "Let's go away for the summer, too. Maybe down to the Keys. I loved it there so much."

"Sure, yes, totally. As long as you call your doctors, and get yourself readjusted." I meant it, too. If she needed me, I could trade a summer on Lake George for one down in Florida, no problem.

I stayed that afternoon. She was in no shape. I fixed her tea and toast. We watched *Titanic*, which was one of our favorite classics. We loved to share a box of Kleenex and hope that maybe this time it would turn out different for Jack and Rose. And I took an evening Amtrak. But I couldn't get that picture of her out of my head, Addy huddled like a lost bird in the middle of this empty loft. And all of that noise in her head that was also charging at her from every wall.

The last thing I did was hug her.

"I promise, I will come back in three weeks. I promise I will go wherever you go this summer. You just have to hang on. Go see your shrink, get your Z levels right, don't put yourself in harm's way, and hang on."

"Promise me again, Lulu," she said.

So I promised again. I promised her a thousand times. "I'll be back here before you know it."

I was really planning to do it, too. One hundred percent. For days afterward, she'd call me on the phone, and make me promise all over again. But I never felt that she believed me.

Last photo of Lucy and Addison, taken in New York, courtesy of Gil Cheba.

MARIE-CLAIRE BROYARD: I went to live in Paris for a couple of months—my impeccable French and my lipstick collection are the only things about myself that I'd consider accomplishments. But I was back by June. I had an invitation to the Artful Awareness fashion show over at the High Line. It's an annual fundraiser, and they'd asked Addison to model.

Now Addison was byoo-tee-ful, but she wasn't what I'd ever call a *natural* model—if you see her in pictures, she never loses her Addison-ness. She stared much too intensely at people. Especially if they were holding a camera. But she was a presence, God knows. And when she kicked down the runway in this punk-rock, deconstructed safari jumpsuit and fabulous scrunchy desert boots, everyone *screamed* with delight. To the untrained eye, Addison Stone was still that same smart, bold, transgressive, sexy girl. Even if you didn't know her by name, you'd probably heard a story. And you could feel that she *was* New York.

I was in the third row. She looked radiant, but afterward when I went backstage, the truth came out. Addison wasn't the meatiest chickadee, but up close she looked, well . . . her bones were protruding, and she had this waxen sickliness in her skin. Maybe it took the fact that I hadn't seen her in a while to know that I was seeing her clearest. Gil Cheba was backstage, too, hovering around her fame like a pesky bloodsucking mosquito. I had to wonder if they were together. I *sincerely* hoped not. But nobody's ever had the real story on that, have they?

Addison was acting odd. She was putting on this stage-y voice. "Oh, Marie-Claire, how was Paris? I have missed you sooo much! We're going out after the show, right? Gil's spinning at Bembe. We'll go in through the side door and get the best table in the back!"

"I'd love to." But I was being fake as well. She wasn't quite *balanced.* She seemed jumpy and her tone was strained. I assumed she was on all the wrong kinds of drugs. Cheba would have given her his last shot of heroin if she'd been inclined toward that vice.

GIL CHEBA: Nobody wants to accept his or her smack on the arse. Nobody wants to take his or her portion of blame for Addison's spiral that summer. Now I might not have heard her signals, but it's a travesty to call me her pusher or her dealer, as all these righteous people will be trying to convince you. Had Addison been partaking of one or two *purely* social drugs at one or two *carefully* cultivated parties—well, who could blame her? She'd had a rotten spring. And there's no doctor who can tell you any antipsychotic medication offers a cure-all.

Zach Frat was still knives-out for Addison. Every day he'd try to find a new way to humiliate her. I know he got her dropped off the lists of the Met's Costume Institute Gala and the Visiunaire party down at Miami Basel. And he'd tell anyone who'd listen about Addison's continued unhealthy obsession with him. Outright lies about her ringing him up in the middle of the night and weeping and begging to get back together. That sort of nonsense.

Lincoln Reed was a wanker, too. He'd completely distanced himself from Addison. So I was never the enemy. I've heard tell all sorts of shit, that I was turning her onto meth or opium. Bollocks. I was a friend and a shoulder to cry on. Rumors can take the piss out, but they won't define me. And in this instance, they simply aren't even close to the truth.

LINCOLN REED: I'd stayed away from her, until I was ready. But I was always in reach—if she'd needed me, I'd have been there. We were both giving each other space. But she sent me a note about Front Street, so I went to check it out one afternoon, sometime in June. It was right after I got back from ten days in Brazil, where I'd ducked off to finish a project. I'd been slightly off the grid. I needed to paint and clear my head. I hadn't even seen Addison since late April—I'd heard she was working hard and partying harder. I also heard Cheba was sticking to her like a cheap suit. Look, I'd heard a bunch of things. I wanted to see her for myself.

I'd texted her before, that I was in the neighborhood, and could I swing by? She texted back yes. Half an hour's warning. She opened the door, and boom—it was as if nothing had happened between us.

"What's up, Reed?"

"What's up, Ads?"

Her smile lit her up. Like always. She was incandescent in that smile. "I want to paint you," she said.

"I want to hold you," I said.

"I want to keep you," she said next, with a laugh.

She looked fragile, but lovely anyway, in one of the vintage smocks she always painted in, long and flowing, spattered, paint speckled on the backs of her hands and all over her beautiful long fingers.

We spent the afternoon together. It was going to happen from the first minute. We weren't broken up. We'd never really broken up, as I saw it. We'd only moved too fast, that was all. We'd moved too fast, and then we'd jumped too far back from the flame. Now we would love and wrestle and pin this relationship back into its right place. We knew we could do it.

I remember being in bed with her, kissing her, staring

down at her face. She was an apparition, a night angel, black hair swirled out on the pillow, her eyes—so twinkling and electrifying. I felt like I'd be burnt up in her heat.

"Let's start over," she said. "But this time, you move in here. With me."

"No." And it was one of the hardest things I ever said.

She just kept looking at me. Crushed.

"I want to see you, of course," I told her. "But I was hurt badly by you. I have to figure out a way to handle us. And I can't be the guy that you're with because you don't want to be alone. That's not the role I see for myself in our life."

She then became incredibly upset, blaming herself.

"Nobody wants to stay with me," she said. "I'm too broken. People see my scars, my meds, and they run. I'm improving all the time, but my failure calls me back." She was crying, and then she couldn't stop. She seemed almost too bewildered. As if her own crying jag had surprised her, a storm that had rushed in without warning. I couldn't have explained it exactly, but I didn't know how to handle it.

I didn't have any words that seemed right, so I just stayed with her, and I held her all night, and at daybreak she said, "It's Lulu's graduation from South Kingstown today. We could take off. Let's drive up to Rhode Island." I didn't want to leave her, and I hadn't seen Lucy in a while, and I'd never been to Addison's home with her, and suddenly this whole day seemed very interesting. So we jumped in my car, and we drove to up to Peace Dale.

LUCY LIM: That morning, I woke up to see that my phone was just lit up in texts:

"We're on Route One!"

"We just stopped at Cumberland Farms for coffee!"

"We're so close we can smell your mom's pancakes on the griddle!"

Oh my God, I squealed! I had the joy dizzies. I'd never in a million years expected Addy to come to South Kingstown High School graduation. And I never in two million years thought it would be the last time that I'd ever see her.

CHARLIE STONE: When my sister came back to our high school that day, I could feel the whole school was almost, like—possessed by it. She didn't look like anyone else's sister. She didn't look like a regular person. She had on this huge black straw sunhat, a little white dress, and this crazy purple scarf that twisted around and around and around her neck and then trailed down along the ground past her ankles. She and Lincoln were as big as two celebrities that we'd ever had. You'd have known they were stars even if you didn't know who they were. Everyone could feel the buzz right from the first second.

After commencement, they were standing around on the school's back lawn. People were shuffling and edging to get near them. And people who didn't even know who my sister was kept holding up their phones, snapping pictures of her. You gotta understand, South Kingstown's a tiny country school where up till a few years ago, the cafeteria doubled as the auditorium. Addison was the shit, the biggest thing that had ever happened, and all my friends—and even people I didn't know—were all like, "Introduce me, introduce me!"

Addison took it really well. After a while, she stuck on a big pair of sunglasses. There was just too much fanzone up in her face.

"Are you okay?" I kept asking.

And I could hear Lucy whispering, "My jeep's right around the corner, Addy. We can scoot anytime."

But Addison was cool. She was signing autographs. Kids were downloading her picture, tweeting her, pawing her, needing to have their moment. She gave it and then some. Maybe it was because Lincoln was standing beside her?

I'd grown up around Addison's ghosts and shadows, and I kept half-waiting for her to bolt. But she was Public Addison that day. She was polished and shiny. And then I stopped being worried for her. I was just proud of how extremely together she was.

We all stopped by the house afterward, so she could check in with Mom and Dad. She didn't stay long. She and Lincoln were leaving to spend the night in Newport. She wanted to go back to Green Hall. She invited me—she really wanted me to come, and if I'd known this was my last time . . . Look, I thought I'd be seeing Addison my whole life. I'd already made plans to hang out with friends. She was a little jittery to be home, too. So I told her I'd come see her in New York. She kissed me goodbye and gave me three hundred dollars. Three mint-condition hundies. I wish I could say I still had 'em, but the next day I went out and bought beer and new basketball sneakers.

ROY STONE: The one who pays the bills is the one who calls the shots. We got a text from Addison that she'd stop by the house for twenty minutes. She didn't want to stay longer. Of course that didn't prevent her mom from running off to the grocery store and spending the whole damn morning slaving over a four-cheese lasagna. We wanted a family lunch. Was that so much to ask? We wanted to share some time with this Lincoln Reed kid, who we mostly knew about from the Internet, and from his interview on *Face the Nation.*

"I'm so sorry, but I can't stay," she said. "I've got stuff."

"Your mother will be so disappointed, Addison."

"Just be grateful for the time that I'm giving. This dump brings back nightmares," she said. Her voice went real hard when she said it, too.

Of course I was upset. That was just a tough thing for Maureen to hear. We owned that house free and clear, too. Plenty of kids can't say that about the roof above their heads. I tried not to let the hurt show on my face. I wanted to protect Maureen. But it was a tough visit. Even with hugs all around just before she left.

And then she was gone.

From: **Addison Stone** <addisonstoneart@gmail.com>
Date: Jun 16 at 3:45 AM
Subject: xoxo
To: Lucy Lim <lucygracelim@gmail.com>

Lulu, wouldn't it be great if every day could be like graduation?
Seeing you graduate—you're done! No more SK!
Bestest day.
I almost felt nostalgia when Dengler-berry hugged me. Almost.
Not really.
She is still such a flippin plastic fake squick.
Whaddaya wanna bet she's pregnant this time next year?

All the glitter dust faded when we got back to the city.
Lincoln dropped me off, and I wanted him to stay the night and he didn't . . .
And after he left, I didn't want to be alone.
Marie-Claire pulled me out to a party, and wouldn't you just know it, but
Zach was there?

So yes.

In answer to your question. What you'd read about online. It happened.

Only it wasn't half as bad as they're making it out to be.

I said stupid things and Zach said worse stupid things.

Cheba tried to throw cold water on it, but I might have had a tiny tantrum.

Wish I hadn't.

I definitely don't regret throwing the plate.

Everyone should throw a plate against a wall at least once in a lifetime.

Zach brings out the worst in me.

And I know Lincoln must have heard about what happened.

He won't answer my texts.

I'm staying in tonight.

No more going out for me for the rest of my life.

Lesson learned.

Sorta.

x!o!

LINCOLN REED: The Rhode Island trip was paradise. We spent the night in Newport. Next day we walked around, strolled over to Green Hall. She took me through how she'd set up *Chandelier Girl*. We ate at the Black Pearl, then we drove to the beach and watched the sun set. It was a fantasy. It didn't feel like reality.

And it wasn't reality. The reality was, I had no room for Addison charging back into my life at warp speed. I was starting something new, a pretty ambitious piece. At the time I vaguely knew it was going to be about urban planning. I'd put up these blow-up maps and aerial views all over my place. That was where my brain was pounding 24/7.

I couldn't have Addison living with me again. Not with all the dreck that blew in with her. Her mess and her fits, her friends and her late nights. And of course there was the Gil

Cheba factor. He was a package deal with Addison those days, and if I suspected I couldn't live with Addison right then, I *knew* I couldn't live with Gil.

That night, after we got back from South Kingstown, I wanted to get home and work. She said that she had work, too. Then Cheba stopped over, and convinced her to head out to some stupid party. The next day, I learned she and Zach had been in a public brawl. It just felt like—okay, here we go again. I was really disappointed.

Zach was a sore spot, always. I didn't need the slings and arrows of seeing their names linked in the press. No way. All I'd wanted was some distance from everything that happened between us.

Addison's bright lights kept leading me back to her. I was crazy to be around her. Especially after South Kingstown. I remember looking over at her, in that giant hat, that giant smile, her huge sunnies that I always teased made her look like a fly, and thinking, *That's the most deliriously wonderful girl I've ever known. I love her. I can't get enough of her.* But I couldn't rescue her. And I felt like the effort had flattened me.

JACK FROEK: "Zach Spat"—that was the headline. Yeah, I was there. Addison Stone was supercharged to the sun that night. She threw more than one plate. She must have thrown six or seven, and some champagne glasses besides. She and Zach destroyed that club.

I hadn't seen Addison in months, not since New Year's Eve. She'd changed. No more elfin girl in the aluminum dress. No more free spirit. The Addison I saw that night was kinetic, uncontrolled energy, and all that anger she had for Zach made her act like him. That night, they were two narcissists fighting for the spotlight. Two spoiled children throwing toys.

DR. EVELYN TUTTNAUER: June 25th. It's in my datebook. A Monday. And the very first phone appointment that she ever missed. Of course I tried to reschedule. I tried very hard. It'd be a violation of my Hippocratic Oath not to have done everything I could at the point when I thought my patient was in crisis.

DR. ROLAND JONES: Addison was very, very good at hiding her illness. She pretended she was swamped with work. She left me long messages where she helpfully suggested multiple times to reschedule our meeting. It would be another ten days before warning bells went off for me. Unfortunately. I think if I hadn't been so hoodwinked, I'd have intervened a lot quicker.

ZACH FRATEPIETRO: Max Berger was making money off Addison. He promised my mother a first look at her next work if she would put a gag order on me. Berger thought her preoccupation with me was getting in the way of her productivity. And so did my mother, apparently.

Did you know, after Addison's and my dust-up, that I was summoned to the house? By my own mother? With her personal assistant present, and my father on speakerphone from Tuscany?

"Happy to do it," I told her. "I'm happy to leave Addison alone. I'm in another relationship."

So irritating. They made me feel like I was twelve years old. I didn't want to be involved at all in this idea that I should have a parental restraining order. It was unprofessional, for one thing. And I just didn't want to have that conversation.

CARINE FRATEPIETRO: Again, I must clarify that my lawyers have asked me not to touch too long on this subject. But yes, of course I hoped that the absurdity between Addison and Zach would fall into the bottom of meaninglessness.

Addison's talent was pushing so hard to the surface. I'd been hearing about this piece called *Bridge Kiss*. Berger sent me a .zip file of images she'd sent of her studies. The faces and forms were no longer traditional representation, and the subject was no longer concrete. The bridge was so dense yet fragmented, the human subjects were fragile yet solid. It was intuitive and thoughtful, nuanced and skilled. She was becoming everything Coulsen had said she couldn't become.

I never like to interfere with the affairs of the heart. I do not like to impose restrictions on my child. But the Addison-and-Zach sideshow had become tedious to everyone. And my son was the one I could claim responsibility for. I love my son, but he is not—how can I put this delicately—a significant person in the art world? His affiliation with Addison was damaging her name, and I'd made an investment in that name. And so I made my wishes very clear.

MARIE-CLAIRE BROYARD: Addison took me out for a sushi dinner. She'd left me a bunch of messages, which wasn't like her. So I made a firm date. I was concerned about her. I had every reason to be. Between the seaweed salad and the hamachi, she confessed she'd been off her medication for about a month. She also told me that Ida was watching her from across the street. I remember my chopsticks slipping from my hands, as I attempted—badly—to hide my reaction. But it was awful to hear.

But I'd known, even before Addison had told me, I'd known in my heart that she'd gone off the Z. I'd probably known at the High Line fashion show, weeks before. No matter that Addison was attempting to give every indication that she was sane. She'd reminded me too much of Mother—the way her gaze had kept darting around, her restless fingers, the way *nothing* she said made a shred of sense. At that dinner, her disconnection was even more pronounced. Her rambling choice of topics, of art she wanted to make and trips she planned to take with her childhood friend Lucy. And television shows, documentaries mostly, that she wanted to create.

She also told me she'd seen all of these psychics, and even a dream interpreter, and these people were smarter than her shrinks. She told me that Lucy and Erickson would have made fun of her for believing. But the psychics had promised that Lincoln was coming back into her life.

"I'm waiting for the right dream, the right way to get to him. Dreams, numbers, sequences—they're all so important, they're the secret, sacred codes of the universe and we never pay attention to them, don't you think, Marie-Claire?"

"It's a lovely idea, darling." As my heart sank. This was not the Addison I knew.

"I'm going back to school," she told me next. And that, I remember, was a comfort. It was just about the only smart thing she'd said all lunch.

"Yes yes yes!" I was clapping my hands. "Go back to school, darling. You can't rely on dreams and psychics. You need so much more than that. Teachers, mentors, new ways to think. It'd be wonderful for you."

But she wasn't even listening. She'd moved onto another ramble. It was very disturbing. I called Erickson the minute I got home.

DR. EVELYN TUTTNAUER: Twice I traveled to New York City, seeking out Addison, who invited me under the guise of appointments that she had no intention of keeping. This after she'd stood up Roland. When I spoke with Roland, we figured maybe the fact I'd come a long distance would reel her in? But no. Both times, she stood me up. She had all but disappeared from Roland's radar, too—though she kept up a running game of phone tag with him.

Of course we were all concerned. I'd left many messages with her parents. I called the Lim family, I spoke several times with Erickson McAvena. I called Arlene and Bill. I even called Max Berger. I recommended to her mother that somebody get hold of her, a family member or close friend, to find out what was happening.

LUCY LIM: Addison knew the plan. First, I had to snooze through two weeks on Lake George with my dad—he counted on that trip too much—and then onward to New York. Addison was working on *Bridge Kiss*, so we were both looking at August as our time. First we'd drive down to the Keys for a week because she'd loved it there so much. We were also talking about going to Nova Scotia. *Anne of Green Gables* was that one childhood book we both agreed on. So this was kind of our dream.

Mom was also away in July, on a little Hawaii trip with some of her girlfriends. Mom and I both knew that Addison wasn't in her best space. We both were on the fence about whether we should just bail on all plans, jump in the car, and go get her.

If only, if only. I'm sure I'll have plenty of other "if only"s in my life, but *if only* I'd gone to see Addy in July—that's the biggest "if only," by which all of my other "if only"s are measured.

CAMERON LUTZ: Addison swung by Paloma's and my apartment one morning in the dead of summer. It was shaping up to be a broiling summer day where you never want to set foot outside, and inside, the clammy-cold air conditioning feels like a thin skin between you and hell. Suddenly, Addison. She hadn't even been to bed yet, she said, and I believed her. She was in her work shirt, and she smelled like stale cigarettes. She looked kind of wild—a forest creature or an elf. She was crazy thin and tired and jumpy. I told her she looked like she needed some sleep and a good breakfast. She said what she really needed was coffee.

So Paloma put on a pot. Then Addison told me to record everything she said, because it was so important. I pretended that I was recording, but I wasn't about to tape Addison Stone's random pontificating. All she started talking about was how we needed a new heist, how the art market was stale, how nothing had value.

After she left, four cups of coffee later, Paloma and I sort of laughed it off, but we were unsettled. We couldn't help thinking back to that first night we'd met her, seeing those scars, and that first picture of Ida that she'd drawn for me. How she'd always seemed too close to the edge, even when she was doing just fine.

I texted Lincoln about it. Just a heads-up. I knew that he still cared about her.

"She can be a nightmare, but she's our nightmare," Paloma said. It was exactly how I felt, too. Then Lincoln texted that he was in back in Brazil, and our hearts kinda went down the drain.

Addison in her apartment, courtesy of Gil Cheba.

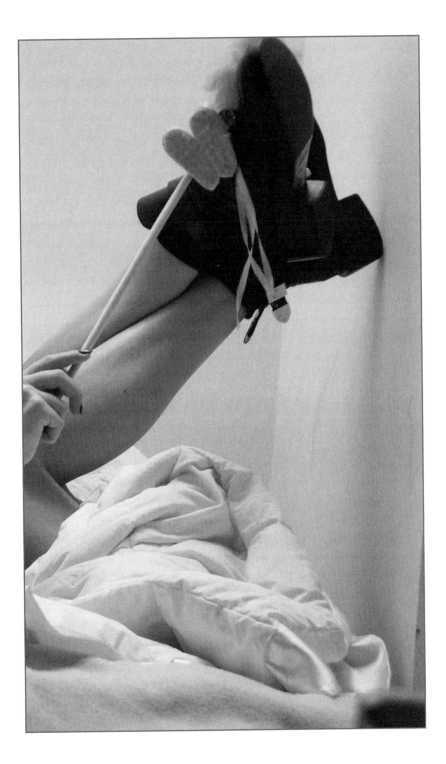

LUCY LIM: I'd pick up my phone, and there'd be sixteen, seventeen messages from Addy. She didn't seem to think voice mail was an obstacle—she'd talk till she heard the beep, call back, and keep talking. She just wanted me to come to New York. That's what all the messages boiled down to. That she was lonely.

I'd landed a job at a hotel resort on Lake George, where I was waitressing my ass off. It wasn't fancy, but I had a life, you know? I was making good tips, and I was dating this guy Marcus—I'm still with him, actually. I guess you could say I was falling in love with him? What I mean to say is . . . at the exact worst time when I had to make a decision, I decided that my life just couldn't be all about Addison anymore.

"Call me at midnight when I'm off my shift," I'd tell her.

But by midnight, she'd have left me six more voice mails. She'd be deep in *Bridge Kiss*, or out with Cheba. She'd phone me at four in the morning. She'd started to talk about Ida, and how Ida had inspired her energy for *Bloody Sophie*. Which prompted me to call Dr. Tuttnauer and Dr. Jones, who were also worried because she'd been phoning them, too, and leaving long messages, even though she'd make excuses not to see Dr. Jones in person, or even to touch in for a real therapy call.

It was hard to explain it all to Marcus. It was bizarre to him that I spent my time talking with my best friend's psychiatric doctors. I saw his point. I didn't want to be consumed by Addison, I wanted to hang out with my guy, and I wanted to earn money, and I wanted to have my summer visit with Dad, and I wanted Addison to not take up the lion's share of my life. I wanted too much, maybe.

GIL CHEBA: She rang me up very late one night that July. She was always calling me that month. She'd caught a dreadful case of telephonitis. Anyway, it was some god-awful time of the night. She was fixated on the idea that a woman was following her. I was barely awake, but I struggled into some clothes, into a cab, over the bridge to Brooklyn, where I found Addison wired and cowering in the corner of her flat. She'd obviously been at work for hours and hours. The whole place smelled like trapped air and stale pizza.

"She just left two minutes ago! She ran down the hall, and now she's up on the fire escape. She's got a knife! Please find her, Gil."

"Jesus, a knife? What the hell, Addison! Who is she? Does she live in the building? We need the cops!"

"No, not yet. Please take care of her—before she kills me!"

Fool that I was, I searched the entire building, floor by floor, my heart jackhamering. It took me well over an hour—I wanted to ring up the cops, but Addison wouldn't have it.

So then I wondered if perhaps Addison was in some sort of trouble with this woman? Or was there any woman at all? Maybe Addison had been given a bad batch of something? I've seen countless people freak out from some illegal potpourri, but I couldn't figure out which cocktail had Addison in its grip. I s'pose it makes a kind of gallows-humor sense that Addison was acting the way that she was because she was *off* her drugs.

I didn't learn until months later that Addison had often rung doorbells and made other people in the complex look for this madwoman, Ida, who had been dead for over a hundred years. I'd been up searching for the phantom of Addison's imagination.

What I will never forget is how Addison's eyes were so fearful. That was why the existence of this person had never crossed my mind. She had to be as real as Addison's fear.

XI.
ALL THE CHILDREN
ARE INSANE.

From: **Addison Stone** <addisonstoneart@gmail.com>
Date: Jul 28 at 4:58 AM
Subject: delete after reading
To: Lucy Lim <lucygracelim@gmail.com>

I got your voice mails returning my calls. But I'm writing back bc I feel
like I've been way too obsessed with the phone.
So I dropped it.
In the trash.
It's still there.
I put the blame on the heat—it was past 100 yesterday. Same today.
Yes yes yes yahtzee, you win.
Because I did go off the Z. I did. But I really think, Lulu, that I'd like to
take a whirl at life without some kind of artificial feel-good in my blood-
stream.
I promise it's been the right-healthy-smart decision for me.
But you are sweet to care.

I'm not hurting the way you think I am.
It feels like a normal. Right kind of pain. Breakup pain. I've got both feet
and my head in the game.
Which is good.
I really want to finish *Bridge Kiss*. My kiss-off to love.
My bridge between where I've been and where I'm going.

Carine saw pictures, and she thinks this is the best work I've ever done. So that's something.

In an hour, Marie-Claire is dragging me to a party.

I haven't been out in a while.

Maybe it's not a bad thing. I should go. I'm sorry for my last 18,000 messages of last week.

Sometimes your voice is all that anchors me to this planet.

x!o! and another x!o! for your mysterious Marcus.

MARIE-CLAIRE BROYARD: There was a terrible heat wave the week of the Fourth, and I decamped to the Hamptons, *imploring* Addison to join me. She'd been my date for a benefit at the Frick, and Cheba had given her some Valium. I knew it wasn't the real Addison. Valium was a poor Band-Aid, but it got her calm, and I wanted to remind her of the big world out here that was just ready to welcome her with open arms.

The *Bridge Kiss* project had truly destabilized her. To the point where the Lutz brothers and I had been emailing a tiny little bit about the possibility of staging an intervention. We just weren't sure what we were intervening in. But we knew she needed help. More help than she was getting.

So I called Carine, and I told her she ought to throw Addison a command-performance party at Briarcliff sometime that very next week before she left for Capri. I remembered that Addison's birthday was vaguely summertime.

Carine said yes to hostessing a big bash up at Briarcliff. Under one condition. "You have to bring Addison personally. I can't throw this party and have her not show, if she's my guest of honor."

I said, "Absolutely no problem!" Inwardly, I must admit, I was *quaking*.

How could I guarantee-deliver Addison?

As it turned out, Addison was receptive to it. Especially when I said I'd come with a team to transform her Cinderella-style. I took a stretch limo over to Front Street that afternoon the next week, with my whole team piled inside—my hair colorist and fashion stylist and my other personal stylists.

"Don't come over till my workday is done," Addison told me.

Well, it certainly wasn't so that she could clean the place up! Good Lord, it looked like a bomb had gone off. Even worse than when she'd *destroyed* Lincoln's loft on Elizabeth last spring. The music was blaring those horrible old organ-wheezing hippie songs, Jim Morrison. Ick, that music always reminded me of weekend dances at Choate.

"You're *covered* in paint," I squeaked at her. "How are you going to scrape it all off your body in time for the party?"

"Oh, it'll be fine," she said. So nonchalant. She seemed a bit spaced out that afternoon, but peaceful and happy. I took it as a good sign. Still, even after two scrub-down showers, flecks of gold metallic and purplish paint were sticking to her skin.

Addison borrowed a shimmery silver-white Viktor & Rolf slip dress. She looked unearthly. Once she was cleaned up, with her hair swept off her head, the white of the dress made the streaks of paint on her hands and legs look as if they were supposed to be there. She really sparkled.

"You're glowing," I said.

That's when she told me she'd spent the entire day with Lincoln Reed.

ZACH FRATEPIETRO: I wanted to come to her party because it made sense for me to attend. It was my mother's house!

And if Addison was there, too, so what? We were all grown-ups. As long as she didn't have any plates to hurl across the room, right? Sure, I had a natural curiosity about seeing her. I always did.

As I was getting dressed, my mother had the nerve to call me. "Zachary, I am instructing you as your mother: do not attend this event. Addison Stone is in no state of mind to see you."

"Sure, Carine."

"I mean it."

"I mean it, too."

My mother was very concerned about Addison, and she wanted to have a look at her. She was also angling to purchase *Bridge Kiss* once it was complete. So that night, contrary to reports that I was there, and even though I'd been known in the past to ignore my mother's warnings, I stayed away. Took some of my buddies out for dinner, and we all were having a great evening. Until Alex called.

MARIE-CLAIRE BROYARD: Briarcliff is Carine's house on the Hudson. It's hideously splendid. Or maybe it's splendidly hideous? First of all, it's still got all the wretched original chimneys and creepy turrets, and a pond surrounded by weeping willows. A vampire palace. My eyes are never used to being dazzled and horrified by it.

Addison had never been there, not even when she was dating Zach. She was fidgety in the car, and she kept checking her phone.

"Lincoln might come," she told me one point. But she said nothing was certain.

I was surprised about all of it. Surprised they'd spent the day together, surprised they'd made a date for that evening. I'd thought Lincoln and Addison were over. But I didn't say anything. I could tell she was hopeful about a reconciliation. She was like a little Fabergé egg perched next to me in the car.

We were a bit late. The sun was just starting to fade. So there were already plenty of other guests, and caterers passing out the champagne and hors d'oeuvres, and there was a jazz trio on the lawn, and my instinct was, "Oh, everything looks perfect, Addison will get over her jitters, she'll forget about Lincoln. If he shows up to this or not, it won't matter."

We walked through the courtyard and inside through this gilded entranceway. And bang, there it was. Like a hostess to greet us. Addison was right beside me, so the painting was also the first thing that she saw. I could feel her, close on my side, just *completely* freeze up.

CARINE FRATEPIETRO: Yes, I obtained the last piece of art that Addison Stone completed. *Bloody Sophie* is a portrait of the actress Sophie Kiminski. It's a gorgeous piece of art. At the time, the buyer had wished to remain anonymous. But let me put the rumors to bed. It's mine. I bought it.

I would have been a fool not to.

MAUREEN STONE: The very last time I ever spoke with my daughter—the night she died—she phoned me from that party. I was at my sister's house in Princeton. As soon as I saw Addison's number come up, well, I had to excuse myself from the table.

Later I learned that Addison had been compulsively talking on the phone to everyone, it seemed—Charlie, me, her friends, her doctors. She couldn't stop. It was apparently an indicator of her psychosis, but nobody knew that she was talking with so many other people, so nobody was really putting the pieces together. I just thought she was lonely. On the phone, I simply couldn't make sense of what Addison was saying.

"Addison, slow down!" I kept saying. "Whatever is the matter?"

All I could gather was it had to do with a painting.

Then Jennifer came into the study. So I kept passing the phone to her, and then she would try to soothe Addison, and then she'd pass the phone back to me, but we couldn't make heads or tails of what was really wrong. It was frustrating.

And Jennifer kept whispering, "Tell her you will talk when she's calm." And eventually I did say that. Of course I wish I hadn't taken Jennifer's advice. Not that I'm blaming my sister, I'm not. Addison was always dramatic.

You cannot fathom my regret, that such a strange and bothersome call from Addison would, in fact, be the last time I'd hear her voice.

LINCOLN REED: We'd been together all that day of the 28th. That morning, I'd flown in and come right over from JFK to her place. Too many people had texted me and emailed me, wanting me to look in on her. It was the first thing I did. Just sent a note I was coming over, and I came over.

"Your apartment looks like a raided terrorist cell," I told her.

She'd been hard at work for I don't know how long. She told me Marie-Claire was coming over later and dragging her off to this party. "I don't want to go. I want to stay in and work."

"So stay in and work."

"I'm the guest of honor. I think everyone wants to check up on me, actually. I've been so buried in *Bridge Kiss*. I probably need some release. So why don't you come?"

"Why don't I drop my stuff, take a nap, swing by here later, and then after the party we go to Sag Harbor?"

Call it my rescue instinct. We both wanted to be together. At the same time, I didn't want to be in her world. I wanted to get away with her. Out of the city, out of the scene, even though I knew it would be a struggle for her to detach from the work, which was hypnotic and beautiful.

"*Bridge Kiss* is us, right?" I asked her. "It's got something to do with our first kiss at the top of the Manhattan Bridge? Right?"

She got shy. "I don't know. It's art. It's that and three hundred million other things."

There are people—Marie-Claire, Erikson, Lucy—who always assure me that she was different around me. Her best self, they always say. But that's not enough for me. I should have seen her better. I should have been my best self. I stayed a while, ordered us some avocado sandwiches and fruit salads, then watched while she ate. And I promised her I'd go to the party.

"Listen, Lincoln, I'm getting through tonight on reserves," she said. "I'm burning out. I need you. All I'm holding onto is that I get to escape with you at the end."

I kissed her. I left her apartment. I went back home, showered, took a nap, went on a bike ride. I was feeling good, hopeful. When I drove up to Briarcliff, at about eight, I saw Addison standing outside. She was in a long white dress against the deep green lawn. She looked beautiful but deeply frightened. She'd lost some of the serenity of the afternoon. I didn't know why. Not at the time. It was, of course, because she knew I'd see the painting.

"Stay out here," she said when I reached her. Her voice was strained and overly chirpy. "The food and music is out here."

"Why, what's inside?"

"Nothing."

"Something."

"No, nothing. Stay out here with me."

"Why do you want me to stay out here?"

"Just because!" She was tugging at my arm. Gripping it. "I want to dance with you is why."

Addison was always a terrible liar.

Eventually, I shook her off. I could feel her watching me, as I left her.

In the shock of seeing it—the painting was hanging right in the foyer so you couldn't miss it as you walked into the house—I had this scrambled idea that I'd been brought to this party just for the express purpose of seeing it. My next thought was that it was such an incredible painting. And then I also saw it as the proof of all those nights that Ads had worked on it in her studio, but never copped to it. How it had become more important than me.

I couldn't decide which was worse; the way portrait-Sophie stared me down, or the way real Addison was looking at me when I came back outside. Her eyes unblinking and filled with unspilled tears.

But I didn't say anything. I just left.

MARIE-CLAIRE BROYARD: My heart was pounding fear. I knew this was bad. Alexandre Norton did, too. Which only upset me more, because I'd mentioned to him earlier that I thought Addison and Lincoln might be getting together again. Every cell in my body was willing Addison to try to stay in control of herself, after Lincoln left.

That's when Alexandre came up to me, smiling like a Cheshire cat. "See that?" he said. "See Lincoln? He was so pissed. The proverbial nail in the coffin."

"Oh, for God's sake. Over one stupid painting? You don't know what you're talking about, Alex," I said.

ZACH FRATEPIETRO: I got a call from Alexandre. He told me that Lincoln finally saw *Bloody Sophie* and that he had just taken off. And so had Addison. But not together.

Honestly, I had no idea. No idea that my mother had purchased this painting. I was in the city at P.J. Clarke's, having beers and burgers with some friends.

"Go to her," Alexandre told me. "She needs you. It's always been you and Addison. This is it. You've got to be there for her."

"Let me think about it."

I'll admit, I was shaky about it. Seeing Addison wasn't what I'd planned to do that night. I finished my burger. Had another beer, and then chased it with a bourbon. Alexandre sent me a text. Go to her.

So I did. When I got all the way downtown, it was pretty late. I stood outside Addison's apartment building thinking, *The fuck am I here?* I wasn't sure if she'd let me in. But she did.

"I wasn't sure I should have come," I said. I was kind of overwhelmed to see her again. Plus I was maybe slightly drunk. Not in fighting shape. I was just so glad to see her. So, so glad, her presence overwhelmed me in waves. She was wearing this long white dress, and she looked like an angel. But when I leaned in to kiss her on the cheek, it was ice-cold, like a corpse.

"Shh. Ida's here," she said, like that explained something. I didn't know if she meant that Ida was inhabiting her or what.

"Oh, yeah? Well, she picked a bad time." I said. Joking,

kind of. I didn't want to get into her Ida world. Freaked me out.

"Your mom either has a terrible sense of humor, or she is clueless," she whispered, sort of laughing, but sort of strange and disconnected and unhappy, too.

"Aw, Addison, it's only a painting. You made it, and you sold it. My mother's a fan. That's always been her worst crime."

"Yeah, I know." She smiled at me. My heart, damn. Just looking at her again.

I'd always believed that we'd find a way back to each other. We'd just gotten ourselves into a really bad patch. Addison had been mine, and then we were forced apart, and we played it out in the press because we both have that kick for drama. It was never as bad as everyone made it out to be.

"Listen, Addison," I said, "maybe we should give us another shot. Isn't Zach-and-Addison what everyone wants, anyway? We're the couple who sells the magazines. Sometimes there's wisdom in the majority."

But I could tell she wasn't really listening to me. She was lost in other thoughts. She'd crawled deep inside her own head. I couldn't have the conversation I wanted to have with her. But she invited me in, and we sat together at her kitchen bar, and it was friendly. She let me poke around, look at her paints and her paintings. She reminded me of other days, better days, when I'd watch her standing at the sink in her Chelsea studio, washing her brushes.

I pretended not to notice that it looked like a tornado had hit her apartment. We'd been angry with each other for so many months. It was amazing to be hanging out with her in a decent, pure way.

Addison's paints/Addison painting, courtesy of Zach Fratepietro.

Except that she wasn't normal, obviously. Something was off. It was the Ida factor, I figured. I'd never bought any of that bullshit, the haunted-girl stuff. But that night, I couldn't shake the feeling that Addison was gripped by something so forceful that, yeah, it almost felt like another presence in the room.

We hung out for a while, she brewed us some tea, and then she tried to ease me out. "Zach, I'm glad you came to see me. But now you've got to go. I need to get my measurements, I need to get *all* the measurements, I need to finish *Bridge Kiss*, and I need to listen to Ida. I never should have left the apartment tonight."

"Imaginary Ida who tried to make you kill yourself? You need to go back to listening to *her*? Don't be insane, Addison."

"Don't be insane," she repeated. Then she laughed. "The

problem is, Ida is the only person who knows me," she said. "She hears me, she speaks to me. She reminds me that the work is the only thing. The work is all that matters. So I've got to get up there. *Bridge Kiss* is an installation, and it has to go up tonight."

"Up where?" I had no idea what she was talking about.

"It needs to be perfect. I can do it without the Lutz boys. I can get to the bridge all by myself."

When I realized she was talking about climbing around on a bridge at night, I was like, "Nope, sorry. Whatever that's about, no way. You're not in any condition to go anywhere, Addison." And then I reached out, and I just took her harness. It was right there, on the coat peg. I shook it at her—I felt like I had to give her some kind of a warning.

"You should go to bed. I'm tucking you in, okay? And I'm taking this to make sure you don't do anything stupid."

She just shrugged. She wasn't bothered by me at all. "You think I need that harness? That's a funny joke, Zach. I wear that harness to be friendly. I wear that so other people think that I care."

I decided that she was bluffing. We finished our tea, and I tucked her in. I guess she was just playing me, but I didn't realize that. I told her I was taking this night as a truce. "Let's get breakfast together tomorrow. I miss you, baby." It was the last thing I ever said to her.

When I left with the harness, I'd gotten her into bed. Even if she hadn't changed, she looked peaceful, with her eyes heavy, like she was about to drop off to sleep. Of course I didn't think she was heading out. If I'd thought that she'd leave the apartment, I'd never have left. If she'd tried to get even close to the bridge, I'd have chased her down.

Why would anyone in her right mind do what she did? Right, I know that answer. She wasn't in her right mind. And I've probably said too much. But whatever, I'm innocent. Taking the harness—that wasn't to goad her. Yes, I was with her that night, but there wasn't one thing that I said that provoked what she did next. Not one thing.

LINCOLN REED: After the party, I drove around to cool my head. In the end, I found myself down on Front Street. I parked and stayed in my car a while. But then I couldn't deal with it. I watched the light from her apartment. I thought about calling her. Then I had a sense that she wasn't alone up there. Cheba, I figured. Or Zach.

I fell asleep in my car. When I woke up an hour or so later, maybe around midnight, I saw that she'd been calling me. My phone kept lighting up over and over like a firefly. I figured whoever had been with her must have left.

I'm not sure why I didn't pick up. I was still angry, maybe. But less so.

She kept calling. Again and again and again. By the time I did answer, she was on the scaffold above the bridge. But she didn't tell me that. She sounded so close in my ear. I heard sirens and the usual white noise. I figured she was just out on her roof or fire escape. She always liked to find the outdoor space.

"I had to run away from the party," I said.

"Me, too. I couldn't deal. I'm so sorry you had to see that portrait that way. Or any way."

"It's all right, it's all right."

"It's not, Lincoln. It's not."

She was saying all of this to me from on the scaffold, which—every time I think about it, makes it all so hard to process.

"I love you, Lincoln Reed," was the next thing she said. Plain and simple. You want to know something? It was the first time she ever said it.

I couldn't say it back. I mean, not on a phone. I should have. Why didn't I just say it? I loved her so much. She was the love of my life. But I didn't.

The cops believe I must have just hung up when she fell. So if she screamed, I wouldn't have heard. I would never have forgotten the sound of that scream. So I'm glad I never heard it. I know without a shadow of a doubt that it was an accident. But if I'd told her I loved her, if I'd said I was coming to join her up there, I know in my heart it wouldn't have happened.

I guess I will always have to think about that.

LUCY LIM: Ida Grimes had such a profound impact on Addy's own life, and yet she was so outside everyone's reach. She wasn't alive, and there was so little information about her. It always itched at me, I was always digging for something, some little nugget about her.

But it wasn't until the summer, after Addison had died, that this nice old lady who worked at the Providence chapter of the New England Historical Society found the newsprint of the death notice, and I learned that the Grimes family lived about ten miles away from North Lyn. The article also said that Ida used to take art lessons from Calliope Saunders. This was likely the "Miss Cal" who'd lived at Addy's grandparents' house.

Attached to the clipping, there was a picture of a girl, posed in exactly the position that Addison had always sketched her.

Ida Grimes photograph. Photo credit unknown; courtesy of Lucy Lim.

MICHAEL FRANTIN: Ginny and I had been married just the year before. We were in New York City for our one-year anniversary. We went back to the bridge, and we were standing right on the pedestrian path. Just holding hands at the very spot where I'd proposed.

GINNY FRANTIN: It was a warm night, with only a breath of a breeze. The girl came spiraling down out of the darkness like a falling star. She must have been all the way up on the scaffolding above us before we even got to the bridge. Suddenly a body was flying down and past us, like Peter Pan. Until she hit the water, I figured it was a daredevil jump, you know? A bungee jump, or that kind of a thing. She was silent, too. Which made it seem more on purpose.

MICHAEL FRANTIN: She was wearing a loose white dress. It billowed out all around her against the night sky. Is it wrong to say that it was enchanting? I'm sure that sounds overly romantic or something, but it didn't look morbid. It looked like a movie or a dream.

LUCY LIM: Lincoln and I always talk about it, how Addy just didn't have that regular human dose of fear. I can imagine that other version so clearly, her toes on the edge, her dark eyes staring deep down into the water, needing to feel the dare. Another day, she might have jumped. But not that night. No, I don't think Addy had organized a jump that night. But I think that when she slipped and fell, she would have decided right then that the accident was, in some way, intentional.

Addy wouldn't have blamed anyone, wouldn't have thought about how we all had failed her, although we had.

She would have pushed as deep as she could have into the experience, knowing that her death was imminent and rising up to meet her—and I bet she probably would have been thinking, "It's a perfect summer night, there's not a cloud in the sky, I told the only boy I ever loved that I loved him, and now I'm hurtling into the most perfect New York death I ever could have imagined for myself."

She would have been consumed only by the absolute beauty of the moment.

If she'd had one regret, maybe, it was that she hadn't paid someone to film it.

AUTHOR'S NOTE

WHILE I WAS WRITING and researching the book, both Lincoln Reed and Zachary Fratepietro were subjects of ongoing criminal investigation with regard to any culpability in the death of Addison Stone. At the time of this publication, Addison's death was ruled an accident. Both young men have since been cleared, and all charges against them dropped.

All artists aspire to a kind of immortality. Like Jean-Michel Basquiat, Keith Haring, Dash Snow, and Francesca Woodman, Addison Stone now seems marked for both death and deity—we see her name and we feel its weight. And yet I hope this narrative has sparked an intimate sense of Addison's life, filled with more scorching creativity than most of us will ever get to experience, even as we cherish, mourn, and remain riveted by her legacy.

Photograph of Addison Stone by Francisco Marin for *ReLive* arts magazine.

ACKNOWLEDGMENTS

ADDISON'S STORY IS A chorus, and I am grateful for every voice that contributed to it. Firstly, for their deep knowledge and understanding of this book's crucial visual art component, I want to thank Alison Blickle, Cat Owens, Fiona Robinson, and particularly Michelle Rawlings, whose haunting portraiture defined Addison's psyche. For her generous counsel from concept to loft space (not to mention her inimitable paint smock), a big thanks to the brilliant Anna Schuleit Haber. As my ethereal Addison, I am so thankful to Giza Lagarce, the perfect face and muse of this character, who also made her invention such a pleasure. Gabriela Bloomgarden, Max Cosmo, Robbie Couch, P. Zach Garner, Richard Holland, Fabian Lagarce, Monica Lagarce, Sara Li, and Evan Richards, thank you all for populating Addison World and sparking it to life. I am of course grateful to my fellow writers and early true believer readers: Michael Buckley, Julia DeVillers, Jenny Han, Elizabeth Kiem, Courtney Sheinmel, Adam Silvera, Bianca Turetsky, and Jessica Wollman—your affirmation is invaluable. I am hugely appreciative of Charlotte Sheedy and Emily Van Beek, as well as the ever-innovative Carly Croll, for such careful watch over this project from start to finish. I can't even add up the hours my indefatigable husband, Erich Mauff, spent thinking through *Addison Stone* with me, but I do know I would not have imagined it nearly as wide and deep and real without him. A big hug for the whip-smart, feisty Soho Teen team; Janine Agro, Meredith Barnes, Juliet Grames, Bronwen Hruska, and Rachel Kowal—what a fascinating journey, thank you so much for all your work to make it happen. Finally, I am indebted to my editor, Dan Ehrenhaft; as a writer, he grasped the strange magic of this book before the first page had been written, and as an editor, he was confident enough let me run with it.